Now Gaia could focus on the real enemy.

She dropped the chair back on the ground and stepped toward Josh.

"Don't," he uttered. "You don't understand what's going on here."

"Oh, I understand exactly what's going on here, Josh, and I won't let it." She took another step toward him, and he took another step back. "No one else is going to die because of me," she explained. "*No one.* You tell him that's *it.* It's *done.*" She took one step closer and Josh lashed out.

"Don't!" he shouted, jabbing his fist forward in a punch.

Gaia dodged the punch and latched both her hands onto his wrist, pulling his weight completely off balance and then flipping him hard to the ground, nearly twisting the entire arm out of its socket.

He let out a painful cry as his spine hit the linoleum, and Gaia couldn't help but take a certain vengeful pleasure in it. Josh deserved absolutely any punishment anyone could devise for him. He deserved so much worse than just to be flipped on his ass.

In all honesty, Gaia truly believed he deserved to die.

Don't miss any books in this thrilling series:

FEARLESS™

Available from SIMON PULSE

FEARLESS™

BETRAYED

FRANCINE PASCAL

SIMON PULSE
New York London Toronto Sydney Singapore

First Simon Pulse edition November 2002

Text copyright © 2002 by Francine Pascal

Cover copyright © 2002 by 17th Street Productions, an Alloy, Inc. company.

SIMON PULSE
An imprint of Simon & Schuster Children's Publishing Division
1230 Avenue of the Americas, New York, NY 10020

 Produced by 17th Street Productions,
an Alloy, Inc. company
151 West 26th Street
New York, NY 10001

Printed in the United States of America
10 9 8 7 6 5 4 3 2 1

Library of Congress Control Number: 2002101036
ISBN: 0-7434-4402-7

To Judy Goldschmidt

Normally I'd be waxing philosophical right now. I'd be going off on some tangent about my childhood or some epiphany I had at Gray's Papaya about how seed-filled orange juice and raw hot dogs were somehow a metaphor for my tragic life.

But really, I'd just be stalling. Mentally stalling. Letting my mind get clouded up with dime-store self-analysis, self-pity, and a bunch of half-baked theories instead of using all that mental energy in a con-structive way. Who knows, maybe even coming up with some kind of plan.

I know. This is something I should have figured out months ago. But it was the look on Tatiana's face tonight that finally woke me up. That numb, defeated expression drooping off her profile as our cab bumped and lurched its way over the potholes on Eighth Avenue, taking our exhausted remains back to the

Seventy-second Street apartment. It was a look I've probably had on my own face a thousand times before. The look of total help-lessness and futility that only *he* could induce.

Loki. The man who may very well be my father. He threatened Tatiana and me with every conceivable fate. He told her that her mother was dead. I could only infer that my father (at least the man I'd always thought was my father) was supposed to be dead, too.

Loki told me he didn't "need" me anymore, whatever that was sup-posed to mean, and then he left *us* for dead, setting his own medical lab—and probably his own entire building—on fire, all the time keeping that same maniacally calm glint in his crystal blue eyes. And what was our response? The only response we could have—to run away. To sulk in a filthy cab and make it back home to lick our wounds, grateful just to be alive.

But I could see it in Tatiana's eyes in the cab. I

could see her doing exactly what I would have been doing, what I probably *was* doing at that moment. What I've done just about every time Loki punctured another gaping hole in my way-too-tattered life. . .

Nothing. Nothing but sulking and pitying and hypothesizing and speculating, which are all a bunch of euphemisms for *nothing.*

And for the first time, I was able to see someone else respond to getting the life sucked out of her inch by inch, to having everyone she loves get shot down like little tin figures in a cheap carnival shooting gallery.

And it woke me up. Because let's face it, I never understand anything when it's happening to me. I never understand all the sadomasochistic stuff I do to myself. But seeing someone else doing it to herself. . . it all becomes so damn *obvious,* doesn't it? Suddenly I can't understand how anyone in her right mind could miss it.

Now I can see it so clearly. *That* is what Loki does to people. That depressive devastation in Tatiana's eyes. That's how he wins. He *talks* people into submission. He buries people with plausible threats until they're almost six feet under.

And it's all lies.

Every single word out of his mouth is complete and utter crap. Tatiana needs to understand that. She can't let herself believe a word he says. And *I* should know. Because I've been letting him mislead me for months. I've bought into every one of his painfully intricate stories. It's so embarrassing, I almost feel like crawling even deeper into my own numbed-over depressive shell. But I'm not going to. Because seeing him start the same game all over again with a brand-new victim, a victim who is fast becoming the closest thing I've ever had to a sister, has finally brought me to my senses.

I won't let him start again

with Tatiana. And I'm through letting him do it to me. The time for helplessness and self-pity is long gone. Sulking and stalling and philosophizing aren't going to do a goddamned thing. Someone needs to stop that poor bastard from lying. Someone needs to shut him up permanently. Whether he's my father or not, someone needs to put him out of his misery.

And yes, in case I'm not being clear, I'm nominating myself for the job.

I'll second the nomination, too, if it brings Loki any closer to dead.

She stood
frozen at
the front
door with
her head **coldness**
tilted
and
forward
like **avoidance**
a marionette
with a broken
string.

GAIA HAD DONE EVERYTHING BUT

Emotional Physics

hold Tatiana's hand as she escorted her down the excessively mauve hallway to the oversized front door of their apartment. It was like walking someone home after some particularly painful surgery. Each one of Tatiana's steps seemed slower and more difficult than the last.

Maybe it was her imagination, but Gaia could have sworn that Tatiana hadn't blinked in the last forty-five minutes. Not since they'd made it clear of the burning building on Eighteenth Street. Not for the entire cab ride home. Her eyes seemed to stay fixed on one particular point somewhere in the distance. Sometimes a few tears would fall from the corners, and sometimes they looked as dry as dead leaves, but they never seemed to close.

Gaia had said it at least five times already, but she knew that she would need to repeat it as many times as necessary until it cut through the black fog that had obviously swallowed Tatiana whole.

"Will you listen to me?" Gaia begged. "Your mother is *not dead*. And neither is my father." Once again Gaia needed a millisecond to convince herself of these facts, but she quickly overcame her doubts. If there was one thing she knew about her father, it was

7

that he'd always been a survivor. And assuming he and Natasha were together wherever the hell they were, she knew he'd make damn sure that Natasha was surviving, too. Besides, now was not the time for Gaia to give in to her ever-growing list of questions about Natasha and her father. Now was the time to trust her instincts and be strong. For herself and for Tatiana. Tatiana was already devastated and confused enough for both of them. It gave Gaia something to fight against. And that was always when she was at her best.

"Can you open your mouth and make *words*, please?" Gaia insisted, trying to find Tatiana's eyes under her sweep of blond hair. "I'm telling you, he's *lying*. Everything he says is a lie."

Tatiana was completely unresponsive. She stood frozen at the front door with her head tilted forward like a marionette with a broken string. Gaia wondered how long Tatiana would have stood there if she hadn't unlocked the door for her. She had to keep trying. Not just to talk some sense into the girl, but to fill in the much-too-depressing silence as they entered the empty apartment.

Empty couldn't even begin to explain it. It was emptier than empty. It was hollow. Tonight the lofty apartment seemed to echo like those filthy tunnels by the West Side Highway. And it was just as black as it was empty. Gaia jumped to the first available lamp and snapped it on, along with any other lamp in the way-too-spacious living room. This was an old ritual for her, part of a three-step plan to counter oppressive loneliness and fill in the silence and darkness. The first was to snap on as many lamps as possible (no overhead lights, since they were more depressing than absolute darkness). The second was to open all blinds, curtains, or shades (particularly at night—streetlights and store lights were far less depressing than sunshine). And the third was to turn on either the TV (preferably MTV, as this would make noise but require no attention) or the radio (a classical station would generally be the best choice since all song lyrics were potentially depressing).

She raced through the three steps, opting for a classical station on the radio, only to find that Tatiana was still standing by the doorway, `staring into her own personal abyss.` She leapt back to Tatiana's side and dragged her to the living-room couch, where she set her down. She then jogged to the kitchen for emergency supplies: Hostess assorted breakfast doughnuts, lime-flavored tortilla chips, and salsa. She dumped a pitcher of water and a mound of coffee into the coffeemaker, flipped it on, and then made her way back to the living room.

She wished she could simply hand over a piece of her emotional armor to Tatiana. If she could just crack off a piece of the old petrified crusty shell that she had formed from five long years of tragic deaths, sadistic

9

lies, and kicks to the chest and head. But it couldn't be done. It went against all the laws of emotional physics. This was clearly Tatiana's first experience with pure unadulterated horror, and recovering from the first time was damn near impossible.

Gaia suddenly found herself flashing back to her own first time. She could hear the sound of gunshots echoing through her old kitchen. She could see the rivulet of blood trickling from her mother's open mouth as her father tried to lift her lifeless frame into his arms. Even then it had been Loki with the gun. It didn't matter if he'd been aiming for her father or not. Either way, one of Gaia's parents had been going to die that night five years ago. And Loki was the murderer. It was always Loki.

She could ward off the depression and anguish, but the anger. . . each additional thought was making it more difficult to keep the anger in check. Every memory, every image of Loki's face, so much like her father's and nothing like her father's. Unless, of course, he *was* her father.

Stay cool, Gaia, she demanded of herself. *Keep your head cool.* She would get to him in due time. She knew that now. She would have to. She was giving in to simple logic. Loki had raised the stakes tonight. She could see it in his eyes as he stood there taunting her from behind a wall of Plexiglas in that eerie lab of his. Something had changed. Until tonight, Gaia had always sensed that Loki wanted something from her, that he had some kind of agenda. But tonight he hadn't seemed to want anything. Except to see her and Tatiana burned to a crisp. He had to be dealt with now. He had to be neutralized, even if only in self-defense.

One thing at a time, she reminded herself. This moment was about Tatiana—about waking her up. Gaia sat down next to her, keeping as much distance as Tatiana seemed to need.

"I *know* him," Gaia said, staring at Tatiana's cold profile. "Loki will say *anything*. He'll say whatever hurts the most. Whatever he's sure will leave you totally incapacitated. But it's all lies, Tatiana. All of it."

"You don't know this," Tatiana murmured, barely even opening her mouth. But at least she'd spoken. That was good. That was something. At least she was past clinical shock.

"I do," Gaia insisted. "I know it. I know him."

"You can't know it for sure."

Gaia paused for a brief moment, because of course Tatiana was right. Especially considering Loki's shift in demeanor. Maybe he had moved past cleverness and deception now. Maybe murder was all that remained of his plan.

"You see?" Tatiana's voice cracked as tears began to flow again from the corners of her bloodshot eyes. "You don't know a damn thing, Gaia. Not a thing."

Tatiana leaned her body into the corner of the couch, curling her entire frame into something resembling the fetal position as she gave in to her tears.

Gaia was at a complete loss. Yes, she and Tatiana had found some mutual respect, and they had begun to forge some kind of familial relationship—but the only thing Gaia could possibly do now would be to hold Tatiana. To cradle her somehow. And that just wasn't going to happen. For one thing, that kind of intimacy would have required removing the thick protective shell Gaia had worked so hard at creating. And for another thing, well. . . that just wasn't going to happen. Not with Tatiana. Not yet. Probably not for a few more years, if ever. But Gaia had to think of something to do for the poor girl.

"Look," she said quietly as she debated what to do with her hands—the ones that should have been hugging Tatiana's shoulders. "Look, we'll. . . we'll *find* her." Tatiana said nothing. She only wrapped her arms around herself, making Gaia feel even guiltier for not being able to provide any kind of physical affection herself. "We'll find them *both*," Gaia promised. "*I'll* find them both."

From out of absolute nowhere, Gaia suddenly felt a shock of emotions crash through her. How many times had she promised herself that she'd find someone—her father, Sam, Mary? How many times had she failed? How many times had she been too late? Tatiana's tears were beginning to break her will, and she knew it.

Tatiana was one of the few people Gaia had ever met who actually seemed to have the same kind of strength as Gaia, the same kind of will. And here she was, curled up in the corner of the couch, crying like a baby. Gaia was beginning to get the horrid feeling that she just might be next.

Thank God for that ringing phone.

Both of their heads snapped toward the black phone on the dining table, mesmerized by its sudden shrill electronic ring. Tatiana leapt from the couch, stumbling over the coffee table and knocking over the chips and salsa as she flew for the phone on the other side of the room. Gaia held her breath and prayed. She prayed that it would be Natasha on that phone. If only to rescue Gaia from the impossible task of consoling Tatiana. Or maybe, just maybe, it could also be her father. Because a few moments more of this unbearable scene and Gaia wasn't sure she'd be able to console herself.

Déjà vu

"MAMA?" TATIANA SQUEAKED, PRAC-tically devouring the phone with excitement. But a moment later her grin diminished. She blew out a stream of heartbroken air and collapsed into a chair at the dining table. But the ghost of a smile did remain on her face. Whoever it was, Tatiana didn't seem altogether disappointed. In fact, whoever it was seemed to possess the one power that Gaia quite surely did not. The power to console Tatiana. The power to make her smile, even if only slightly.

"Ed," she sighed, curling up with the phone like it was keeping her warm.

Gaia cringed and turned away. She turned away for a whole slew of reasons. For one thing, watching Tatiana coo like a lovesick bird at the sound of Ed's voice was both confusing and sickening. Tatiana had made it clear that she and Ed were simply not going to happen. It was officially a nonissue. But Gaia felt deeply uncomfortable nonetheless. No, not just uncomfortable. Sick. Sick from not being with Ed every waking moment, as the deepest and most real part of her had wanted to so badly for days. Sick from having to be so cold to him in order to protect him from Loki. Sick at the thought of him making anyone but her smile.

And then it got even more confusing. She felt sick because no matter how badly she wanted Ed, she shouldn't have been as kind as she'd been to him these last couple of days. It could only put him in more danger. Especially considering how increasingly deranged Loki was becoming by the hour. But how could she have helped it? He was *walking,* for God's sake. How could she not celebrate that with him?

"Ed, I am *so glad* to hear your voice," Tatiana said. "You have no idea how much I needed someone to. . . *what?*"

Gaia turned back when she heard the sudden shift in Tatiana's voice. The smile had dropped completely from Tatiana's face now, and her eyes drifted to meet Gaia's. Gaia could see another tear beginning to form in her eye as she slowly let the phone dangle from her hands and then fall to the table.

"What?" Gaia asked, narrowing her eyes as she rode a fine line between concern and confusion. "What's wrong?"

"Nothing is wrong," Tatiana murmured, looking even more depressed than she had before. "He wants to talk to you."

"What?"

"You heard me," Tatiana said, dragging herself back to the couch and curling up as far from Gaia as possible. Boy, did she have the guilt trip mastered. "He says he needs to talk to *you.*"

"Well. . . I can't," Gaia said, darting her eyes over to the receiver on the table, wanting so badly to grab it and hear his voice for just a few seconds. But that was the absolute opposite of what she needed to do. She needed to double her coldness and avoidance to make up for the day's mistakes. She needed to cast him way, way out again, back into the world of safety. "Tell him I can't."

"He says he *has* to talk to you," Tatiana mumbled. "*Now*. Emergency, he says."

Gaia stared at the phone a few seconds more and then ran to grab it. She'd have to set him straight now. She'd have to send him an ice-cold message to leave her the hell alone. And maybe. . . listen to his voice for a few seconds.

"Ed, listen to me," she barked. "I made a big mistake by—"

"Gaia, listen," Ed interrupted with an oddly grave tone to his voice. "I'm at the hospital. St. Vincent's. It's Heather, Gaia. Something's happened to Heather, and—"

"What?" Gaia cut him off. "What do you mean? What happened? Did someone—"

"She wants to talk to you, Gaia," Ed interrupted again, sounding so disturbingly serious. "She wants you here *now*. Just you and me, she says. Can you get here immediately? You've got to get here now."

Gaia was at a complete loss for words. Except for the one word that had suddenly begun to sting her brain. *Josh*.

Josh had hurt Heather somehow. That's what it had to be. Just like Gaia *knew* he would. And Gaia had done nothing to stop it. Sure, she'd tried to talk some sense into Heather, to warn her, but Heather seemed to have given in completely to some kind of chemical imbalance. She'd succumbed to these weird fits of violence and paranoia and all kinds of bizarre delusions of grandeur.

But Gaia should have cut through it somehow. She could have cut through it. She was strong enough.

Déjà vu had never felt so sickening. Gaia had been through all this before with Heather. There had been another chance to warn Heather all those months ago—to *save* her, and she'd completely screwed that one up, too. She'd let her own pride get in the way, and it had ended up getting Heather slashed in the middle of Washington Square Park. And now here they were again. Heather was back in the hospital, and *somehow,* one way or another. . . Gaia knew it was her fault. Again.

She managed to control the overwhelming wave of guilt washing over her long enough to answer Ed's question. If Heather wanted Gaia there, then Gaia would be there. She absolutely deserved every bit of punishment that Heather wanted to dole out, which was surely why Heather wanted so badly to see her.

"I'm coming," Gaia said, a cold chill running down her back. "I'm leaving now."

"Okay," Ed said. "I'll tell her."

The phone went dead before Gaia could say another word. Oh God. Ed must hate her even more than Heather did. He and Heather must be sitting in that hospital room cursing the day Gaia Moore set foot in that school. And they'd have every right. The Curse of Gaia Moore had spread like a deadly virus to the far reaches of Gaia's world. She was responsible for

17

all of it. So many people's pain. Now she was just praying that Heather would be okay—that she could survive the curse.

"I have to go," Gaia said, rushing for the door.

Tatiana flashed her a pained glance.

"It has *nothing* to do with me and Ed," Gaia assured her. "I swear." Gaia wanted to bring Tatiana with her, but Ed had made it abundantly clear that Heather only wanted to see Gaia, and Gaia wanted to be damn sure to respect Heather's wishes. *Too little, too late,* she chided herself as she opened the door. Still, something felt very wrong about leaving Tatiana alone in the house.

"Look," Gaia said, trying to figure out some way to bring her along. "Do. . . do you want to come with me?"

"No," Tatiana mumbled, keeping an entire couch cushion pressed to her chest. "I want to stay here. I don't want to move. You do what you have to. . . ."

"I swear this isn't about Ed," Gaia said again, trying to figure which person in her life was making her feel the guiltiest right now. It was a tie. Between all of them. "I'll be back as soon as I can."

"Just go," Tatiana said.

"I'm *going.* Just do me a favor, okay?"

"What?" Tatiana grunted.

"I want you to lock the door," Gaia said. "I want you to lock all the doors, close the shades, and steer clear of the windows, okay?" Tatiana didn't answer. "*Okay?*" Gaia pushed.

"Okay," Tatiana agreed reluctantly, curling up even further.

"Okay," Gaia said more calmly. "I'll be right back."

She closed the door behind her and headed for the stairs. But she stopped in the middle of the hallway and waited until she heard Tatiana lock the door. It gave her at least a moment of relief. But only a moment. Because the facts were still the facts.

Gaia and Tatiana had nearly died, and Heather was in the hospital. Loki's mind games were over. He was way past his convincing double-talk and his cryptic little schemes. Sometime in the last hour. . . he'd gone on the warpath. Either that or he'd lost what was left of his mind.

LO and behold, it is true. We are in fact wasting the majority of our lives. I suppose I'd always had my suspicions, but I was never sure until now. Yes, I have given myself one very simple injection, and glory, hallelujah, I have seen the light.

You want to know the truth? You all might as well be locked up in pods and cocoons until the auspicious day when everyone will be able to inject themselves with 20 ccs of phobosan II. Because until that day, let me tell you what your life will consist of.

Absolutely nothing. Oh, you will surely convince yourself that it is something. But believe me, as long as you feel fear, your life is nothing.

You see, one day you will take the shot, as I have, and you will wake up, and you will realize that the life you were leading—a life with fear—is the human equivalent of living in a Roach Motel. You, good citizens of Now, are human cockroaches. Stuck in a brown cardboard box, staring out at the light and convincing yourself that with just a little more effort, you'll reach that light, totally unaware that your fearful little legs are absolutely glued to the ground.

And so you will dream of the light, and you will imagine yourself reaching the light, and you will plot out your little road to the light. You will even convince yourselves that if you don't reach the light in *life,* then, of course, you're sure to see the light in *death.* How very tragic, don't you think? How miserably, miserably sad.

You must understand: That glue that is holding your little insect legs to the ground. . . that is fear.

Fear is the reason you're still in that pathetic little town. Fear is the reason you're still in that miserable job and that horrible school. Fear is the reason that you are poor and unsuccessful and unpopular. It is the reason you are ugly, the reason you are stupid. It is the reason you are nothing.

Because you won't let go. You won't face the facts. You won't *free* yourself from the glue.

Dr. Glenn has obviously perfected the drug, as this second generation of phobosan has left me in a state of utter euphoria without one single side effect to show for it. There are none of the violent tendencies we were seeing in subject B. None of those hideous outbursts and uncontrollable spasms the Gannis girl was exhibiting. Just complete and unadulterated clarity. The only thing that shot of phobosan has done to me is wake me from a lifelong sleep.

I realize now that I have been holding on for so long. Absolutely mired in glue. And now, with my fears cast aside, I am ready to let go.

All this time, each and every one of my plans had been failing for one very simple reason. I was trying to carry out every plan without losing Gaia. I'm no longer ashamed to say it now. I'm no longer ashamed to say anything.

I was afraid of losing my daughter.

Just as I had been desperately afraid of losing Katia. I had convinced myself that I could not live without Gaia, I could not live without my daughter's love.

Glue. Nothing but glue.

You see, this fearless blood that is now running through my veins. . . that's the only part of Gaia I need now. All I wanted was to bring my daughter back into my life—to make her a part of me again. And I've done that. I now have bits and pieces of Gaia inside me. But ironically, it's really my daughter's fearless genes that have helped me free myself of her. Until now, I've just been too afraid to admit what I've really always known.

I will never win her over. Gaia is *never* going to love me. *Never*.

You see how *easy* it is without fear to nail me to the ground? The simple truths! The beautiful truths that will be my freedom and my salvation! Katia is long gone. And the child we shared will never love me.

The conclusion here is so obvious, I cannot even fathom how many years I've wasted avoiding it. *I don't need her anymore.* I don't need anyone. You see, I am finally capable of doing what every one of you would be far too afraid to do. I am starting my life from scratch. I am going to eliminate all the chaff from my life—all the painful glue that has kept me paralyzed, and then I will finally move on. Straight into the light.

I will no longer fear dead ends. There are no dead ends. There are other women for me to meet, and when I meet the right one, we will have new sons and daughters of our own. And perhaps those sons and daughters will be even more special than Gaia, given my new genetic makeup. And that woman, and all my sons and daughters. . . they will all love me the way I should have been loved in the first place—by my brother, by Katia, by Gaia. I know this now. I can believe it one hundred percent because there is no fear to taint that belief.

Yes, it is time to close out the entire fearful chapter of my life. I see now what I must do. In order to start the new, I must first destroy the old—rid myself of the glue. So I suppose this will be my last good-bye to everyone that I'll need to eliminate—everyone who has kept me stuck in this fearful and unsuccessful stagnant void. Good-bye, Tom and Natasha. Good-bye to the Gannis girl and Gaia's young friend Tatiana.

And good-bye, my dear Gaia. The world will be a much smaller place without you in it, but speaking as one fearless person to another, I know you understand what I must do.

It is time to wipe the slate clean.

"FIRST AND FOREMOST, CONGRATULATIONS
are in order." Loki offered his most generous smile as he turned to Dr. Glenn and his other mild-mannered colleagues in white lab coats. The single exposed lightbulb hanging down from the ceiling was just bright enough to illuminate their grateful if somewhat reserved smiles.

Nine-Millimeter Automatic

"I know I can be quite demanding at times," Loki went on, making brief eye contact with each of the dimly lit doctors on the team, "but perhaps now you can all see why I have been so demanding. Phobosan II is an unequivocal victory, and for that, I commend you all. I only wish you could experience its remarkable properties firsthand, as I have."

"Sir, if I might," Dr. Glenn interjected, the smile still pasted across his face. "I am a bit concerned about your decision to volunteer yourself as the test subject for the second generation. We really haven't been able to fully test the drug, and I'd like to—"

"Oh, I appreciate your caution, Dr. Glenn," Loki interrupted, "but I assure you, you are selling yourself short." He stood up out of his tattered black leather chair and moved closer to the doctor, staring into his eyes with sharp, pointed confidence. "Look at me, Doctor. I think I'm far from a 'test subject.' The testing stage is clearly over. No kinks, no side effects, not even any *mild* side effects. Unless, of course, you consider supreme confidence and total clarity of mind side effects. I'm not even sure you understand how profound a victory this is. We've done so much more than just concoct a fearless serum here."

"Well, sir, I know that *right now* you may be feeling quite—"

"Doctor, I assure you, you have *no idea* what I am feeling right now. You might understand if you or your staff had even a fraction of my courage and were willing to take the injection, but I suppose that's the irony, isn't it? You're all too afraid to be fearless."

Loki turned from the doctor and took a few steps back from the group to address them more officially. "Now, enough of the congratulations," he announced. "Let me move on to *apologies.* Because I owe one to each of you."

Loki watched as the faces before him took on varying degrees of confusion. Looking particularly baffled were the two matching faces to his right—the faces of QR1 and QR2—the two remaining genetic clones of Josh Kendall. Of course, their DNA was now the only thing that remained of Josh, as Loki had been forced to terminate the real Kendall. The boy's feelings for Heather Gannis had led to him to be quite stupidly disloyal, and Loki had been left with no choice but to eliminate him. Normally, having to look at these two identical images of Josh's face would only frustrate Loki further, but with phobosan II coursing through his veins, nothing so trivial was going to faze him.

"Apologies?" QR1 asked with that same insistent tone that had begun to make Josh such a nuisance. "Apologies for what?" Apparently their faces weren't the only things that were identical. It seemed one could clone an attitude as well.

But they did have every right to be confused. Loki knew that his staff wasn't at all accustomed to hearing him apologize. After all, he had always made it quite clear that *they* were the ones making all the mistakes. But now he had come to realize a certain ignorance in that perception, and he felt compelled to set the record straight.

"Well, for a couple of things, actually," Loki replied. "First of all, I'd like to apologize for the rather shoddy surroundings." He opened his arms slightly and referenced the grayish-white walls and the dark, creaky floors of the five-story Brooklyn brownstone. He'd left all the splintered wooden floors unfinished and put in no furniture other than a few absolutely necessary secondhand items.

"I know these are not the kinds of accoutrements you are used to, but I assure you, this is all we're going to need. We're not going to be here for very long, and when we leave, that is when we're going to want to dispose of the furniture and clean the floors of evidence."

A few members of Dr. Glenn's team averted their eyes. The word *evidence* clearly made them uncomfortable.

"But much more importantly," he went on, "I want to apologize to all of you for. . . well, for making a mess of things, really."

Now his audience looked downright shocked. "You can all stop gawking now," he said, smiling. "It's true. I have made a mess. And I'm quite sure that more than a few of you have whispered as much behind my back. The truth is, I've been wasting so much of our time pining for Gaia's love and affection when in fact, `all we ever really needed... was her blood.` So, from this point on, I assure you, blood is the only thing we are out for."

The silence in the room was deafening. His unusual degree of bluntness had apparently left them all speechless. "The logic couldn't be simpler, really," he explained. "When one makes a mess, the only solution is to clean it up, and that is why, as of 9 P.M. this evening, Operation Clean Slate will commence. We have finally found success with phobosan II, but the road to that success has been littered with witnesses and enemies, and that simply won't do. All of them will need to be cleaned out within the next forty-eight hours. That is our deadline. Once the last of the mess has been wiped up, we'll be leaving this filthy city for quite some time and moving on to far greater things. Now, thankfully, some of the mess has already been taken care of—George Niven, Josh Kendall—"

"What?" QR1 blurted, shooting up from his flimsy folding chair. "What are you talking about? What did you do to Josh?"

Loki turned to QR1 and locked eyes with him. He had no time for attitude. "I just *told* you what happened," he explained calmly, staring QR1 into submission. "Your 'brother,' Mr. Kendall, has been cleaned. He attempted to betray me, not to mention everyone else who has worked so hard on the serum. If he had succeeded in administering the counteragent to our first test subject, Ms. Gannis, we might never have completed the testing of phobosan I. His betrayal left me with no choice but to terminate. Do you have a *problem* with that?"

Silence filled the dimly lit room again. The one stark bulb suddenly seemed to cast an interrogationlike light on QR1 as Loki watched this carbon copy of a young man have a most unexpectedly emotional reaction to Josh's death. There seemed to be a genuine sense of loss in his usually inhuman neon blue eyes. Loss, and sadness, and even a tinge of deep resentment as he and Loki stayed locked in a visual showdown.

Loki was of course being facetious when he referred to Josh as QR1's 'brother.' A clone couldn't truly have a brother. How could he have a brother if he didn't even have a mother? This was what made QR1's reaction all the more curious. But now was not the time for curious. There would be plenty of time for curious once this operation was complete.

"I just don't see. . . ," QR1 began. "I don't see why you had to kill—"

"Before you answer," Loki interrupted coldly, "I suggest you take a look at QR2 and try to emulate his behavior." QR2 was still sitting quietly in his chair, indicating no emotion whatsoever. "Is that clear? Now, are you going to sit down. . . or are you going to add to the mess?"

Loki reached inside his coat and wrapped his hand tightly around the handle of his `nine-millimeter automatic`, hoping to speed up QR1's reply by simplifying his options. But there was no need to even remove the gun from its holster.

"I. . . I'm sorry, sir," QR1 uttered quietly, dropping back down into his chair and wiping any traces of emotion from his face.

Loki waited one more discomforting beat before removing his hand from the gun.

"Fine," he said finally, scanning the room for any further dissidence. "Then let's dispense with the congratulations and apologies and begin going over this operation. Forty-eight hours should be plenty of time, but I'll need you all to follow my instructions with absolute precision. As I'm sure you all know, each one of these messes will require an entirely different method of cleaning."

A kick to
the gut from
one of
Loki's thugs
would **aimless**
be a
holly jolly **eyes**
Christmas
memory
compared to
this.

WHY WAS SHE ALWAYS RELIVING

Twisted Catharsis

the worst memories? Why couldn't it ever be a memory of that trip to Cape Cod with her parents or that cup of Godiva hot chocolate with real whipped cream that she and Ed shared three months ago at Balducci's? No, it was always the horrors that repeated themselves. The mistakes and the accidents and the World's Most Painful Moments. Right now Gaia could think of a thousand other experiences that would make for a preferable déjà vu. Reliving last year's dental surgery would certainly be a treat. A kick to the gut from one of Loki's thugs would be a holly jolly Christmas memory compared to this.

Because this moment—this walk of shame through the cold white linoleum halls of St. Vincent's Hospital. . . this was the déjà vu from hell.

Everything was exactly as it had been the last time Gaia visited Heather in the hospital. The same stink of ammonia, the same garbled voices barking over the PA system, the same phantom faces of the sick floating by in wheelchairs, making Gaia feel guilty for even being able to walk. And once again Gaia was trying to form the appropriate apology to Heather in her head, knowing all too well how meaningless it would be. At least this time the entire senior class of the Village

School wasn't lining the hospital halls, staring at Gaia like she was the class Antichrist for letting Heather get slashed. But it didn't really matter if they were there or not because Gaia could still feel them there. She could still feel their eyes ripping her to pieces for being so cold and heartless.

After all, her mistake was, for all intents and purposes, the exact same one it had been the last time. The same mistake that she'd already spent most of the evening punishing herself for: saying nothing. That night all those months ago when she'd run into Heather, that was the one time in Gaia's entire life that she *hadn't* opened her big mouth. And that's all it would have taken. Just one sentence. Just a few words of warning to Heather about that gang of sicko skinheads waving their knives around inside the park.

And it was really just the same with Josh. Sure, she'd tried to warn Heather about him, but what was that really worth? It took a whole lot more than words to deal with Josh Kendall, and Gaia knew that. She should have just sought him out herself and dropped him down a manhole, but she'd been too busy being trapped in her own succession of nightmares. And yes, Heather's new obsession with trying to pick a fight with Gaia had been a most bizarre and troubling pain in the ass. But if Gaia had taken any real time to think about it, she would have considered the likely possibility that Josh had just been systematically driving

Heather crazy. Just like he'd done to Sam. Just like Loki tried to do to everyone else.

Loki. It always led back to Loki. There was simply no one else on this planet with such an uncanny ability to infuriate Gaia or make her despise herself. At least that was what she thought. Until she opened the door to Heather's hospital room and saw Heather's family.

In case Gaia hadn't learned it already, here was a very valuable lesson: No matter how bad she felt. . . she could always feel worse.

The moment she opened the door, it felt like the fluorescent lights in the room had suddenly gone to black and a glaring white spotlight had nailed her against the wall. Heather's entire family was seated around the bed, staring at Gaia, boring holes through her skin with their eyes. Of course, she was the absolute last person the Gannis family would have wanted to see right now. As far as they were all concerned, they were staring at the girl who was responsible for the near murder of their beloved sister and daughter.

Heather's father's jaw was clenched so tightly, Gaia thought he might never be able to unlock it again. Her sister Phoebe's gaunt face and dark accusing eyes made her look like some kind of vengeful ghost. And then there was Heather's mother, whose rage toward Gaia was so laser focused, it sent her two steps backward. But Gaia couldn't allow herself to leave yet. After all, she still had more hatred to face. There was Ed, who was staring at her like she was in a police lineup. And then there was Heather. . .

Gaia couldn't even begin to read the expression on her face. Her eyes seemed so hauntingly blank—just staring aimlessly into space as if she couldn't bear to look directly at Gaia. As if Gaia weren't even in the room. Somehow, that hurt so much more than the vicious glances from Ed and Heather's family. At least there was some kind of twisted catharsis in being actively hated. But for someone to hate you so much that they couldn't even acknowledge your presence?

"Who's there?" Heather asked in a raw scratchy voice. She was staring just over the top of Gaia's head. "Is that Gaia?"

Gaia had no clue how to respond. Was this Heather's immature way of insulting her? Was she playing some kind of I'm-ignoring-you game like she probably used to do in the third grade? Gaia looked to Ed for answers, but all she got from him was that same accusing stare, until he finally turned back to Heather.

"Yeah," he said quietly. "That's her."

"Gaia. . . ," Heather uttered. "You came."

"Yeah," she replied, taking a step closer to the foot of Heather's bed, trying to ignore the Gannis family firing squad. "What. . . what happened?"

"I'm not sure," Heather said, still staring off into space.

"Heather. . ." Gaia darted her eyes to Ed and the

family before turning back to Heather reluctantly. "Heather, why won't you look at me?"

The entire family bowed their heads with discomfort, as if Gaia had just asked the one question she wasn't supposed to ask.

"Because I can't see you," Heather replied, coughing out a horrid, nervous laugh. The laugh immediately died as narrow tracks of tears began to fall from each of her aimless eyes, dripping onto her bleached white pillowcase. "I can't see anything."

HOW LONG WAS I ASLEEP?

Dead Air
Tatiana pressed her hands to her face, grinding her palms against her barely open eyes, trying to stretch her body out of its contorted fetal position on the couch. Apparently the hours of trauma had finally caught up with her and she'd cried herself to sleep. Now everything just throbbed. Her limbs, her eyes, her brain—they were all throbbing.

She slid her aching body slowly from the deep dent in the couch and stumbled back to the phone. Maybe her mother had called? Maybe she'd left a message and Tatiana had slept through the entire thing...?

The red digital zero on the answering machine looked twice its usual size. She knew no one had called. She could have been in a full-fledged coma and she still would have jumped from that couch if the phone had rung. Awake or asleep, she was still praying every ten minutes for her mother—screaming silent little prayers that were clearly falling on deaf ears. Any sign would do. An anonymous ring of the phone, a blank letter in the mail, just the slightest hint to indicate that her mother was alive, that she was still out there somewhere, that Loki was the goddamn liar Gaia swore he was. . .

But there was nothing. Nothing but stale dead air crawling through the much-too-spacious apartment. And that horribly depressing classical music station still cranking out tinny piano concertos that made the house feel like some dank eighteenth-century mausoleum.

"Shut up," she moaned, clamping her hands over her ears. She lunged for the stereo and slammed her hand on the power button, slapping the entire stereo back against the wall as silence finally filled the room.

This is not a funeral, she told herself. *Not yet. . .*

But now the silence was unbearable. Tatiana's eyes drifted around the empty living room as she realized just how alone she was in this house. Just her and the world's loudest ticking clock. And a pitch-black hallway across the room that led to nothing but more dark and empty rooms.

But then the miracle came.

A sound. A sound that Tatiana hadn't made herself. A sound that wasn't the ticking clock. This sound was coming from the *front door.* Her head snapped toward the door just in time to see the brass doorknob begin to twist from side to side. Only one thought consumed her brain.

Thank you. Thank you, God.

She leapt for the door and flipped the top bolt lock open. "Mama," she called out. "Mama, is that you?" She placed her fingers on the bottom lock.

And then she froze.

Gaia's warning had come rushing back to her. "Lock all the doors," she'd said. "Stay away from the windows. . . ."

"Tatiana, please. . ." A man's voice suddenly whispered through the door, causing her to jump slightly. He sounded utterly desperate. "Open the door, *please.*" She felt the doorknob twist again in her hand.

"Who is it?" she shouted back nervously. "Who's there?"

"Shhh. Keep your voice down," the alien voice insisted. "Loki's people are out there. They're probably watching you right now. Please. I'm trying to help you. I know where your mother is. She's alive." He shook the knob again.

"Where is she?" Tatiana demanded, her heart rate quadrupling. "Where is my mother?" She pressed her eye to the peephole, but the man seemed to be crouched out

39

of range, shaking the knob with more and more force.

"I'll *tell* you," he promised, "I'll tell you where she is. I'll tell you everything, but you've got to let me in. Please, just *open the freaking door*. Oh, Jesus. . . Loki's people are coming. . . . They're coming. . . . They're—"

The bottom lock clicked open right before Tatiana's eyes.

Her brain hollered an instant warning: *Move. Move now or—*

But her body lagged too far behind. The door was brutally forced open right into her face, ramming her forehead with a hundred pounds of cold industrial metal and knocking her straight off her feet. Everything went completely black. Her head bounced off the hardwood floor like a volleyball that had just been spiked at eighty miles per hour, leaving her brain vibrating inside her skull.

She was stuck in a pitch-black tunnel, her eardrums cracking from the high-pitched ringing deep inside her head, the rest of her body paralyzed with shock.

She forced her stinging, dysfunctional eyes open just in time to see him. From her hazy perspective on the floor, he looked just as tall as the ceiling. He was towering over her like a cold black monolith, a black ski mask over his face and a lock pick in his black-gloved hand.

"They're *here*," he announced, slamming the door behind him and dropping his pick to the floor.

Tatiana's heart froze. Her hands and feet went numb and her body locked completely as she lay helpless and bathed in debilitating pain on the floor. A thought swept across her mind like a quick gust of icy wind: *I'm going to die.*

The intruder leaned down to her paralyzed body, the black mask zooming toward her face, and finally a hint of her adrenaline kicked in. She let out a deafening screech and flipped herself over, clawing her way desperately across the floor. But his massive hands took her arms from behind, raising her petite frame into the air and slamming her back against his chest, knocking every ounce of air out of her lungs.

"Just shut up for two seconds, all right?" he whispered into her ear. "All I need is two seconds here. Just two seconds. . . and it'll be over."

Tatiana flailed every limb to break free, but his tight grip was making it impossible to breathe. She opened her mouth for her loudest and most desperate scream yet, but she was suddenly unable to utter a sound.

He'd wrapped a cold strap around her neck. And he'd begun to pull on that strap with maximum force, yanking her head back against his shoulder, cutting off every ounce of her oxygen as he twisted tighter and tighter, strangling her without mercy.

"Don't fight it," he said calmly, his fists tightening even further. "Just let go. Let go. . . ."

She could feel all the blood vessels in her face

constricting from the strain. She kept trying to dig her fingers under the strap, but it was too tight. Breath was impossible now. She needed to breathe in. Her body *needed* to breathe in, and she couldn't. Not even the beginning of a breath. Only the horrid, dizzying feeling of strangulation as her eyelids began to flutter from complete oxygen deprivation.

The room grew dimmer. She could still hear him in her ear, telling her to relax, telling her to stay quiet and let go, but his voice grew fainter and fainter, rumbling and buzzing with horrid echoes and distorted static. All she could hear now was her own voice in her head. Her own voice howling at her in a rage.

Is this how you want to die? Is this where you want to die? In this empty apartment in this filthy city? Alone? Fight, you pathetic little weakling. Wake up and fight!

And finally she did just as her attempted murderer suggested. She stopped struggling like a dog on a leash and "let go." That way she could focus all her remaining energy into her right leg, which she raised slowly from the ground. With all the force she could muster, she kicked backward, slamming the heel of her shoe straight into his crotch.

"*Ugh,*" he gurgled, doubling over to the ground as the strap fell to the floor.

No time to think or recover. No time to breathe. Tatiana whirled around and laid into his curled-up body with a series of wild vengeful kicks until she saw blood. She turned and stumbled quickly toward the kitchen, gasping for the massive amounts of oxygen she'd lost. She slid past the refrigerator and collided with the counter, reaching to the right of the sink and pulling the largest steel knife from a set of ten. She ran back to the living room, but before she'd even scanned the room, a sharp kick had knocked the knife from her hand and another had knocked her face forward to the ground.

"You stupid *bitch*," he hollered. "I tried to make it easy for you! You want to make it ugly, fine." He leaned to grab for her again, but this time, thank God, there was no paralysis.

Tatiana spun onto her back and kicked her feet out straight into this chest, knocking his six-foot frame back against the living-room wall with a thud. This left him disoriented long enough for her to grab the knife back up from the floor. He lunged for her again but stopped himself short just before her defensive thrust of the knife punctured his cheek.

"Whoa, there." He laughed, holding up his arms. "Watch where you point that thing."

"Get out!" she screamed, thrusting the knife at him again and again as he backpedaled slightly. Now that they were face-to-face, she was suddenly struck by the disturbing image of his bright blue eyes peeking out from behind that murderous black ski mask.

"You get out of here or I swear to God, I'll drive this straight through your heart and pin you to that god-damn wall! Get out! I'm calling the police!" She moved back cautiously toward the phone, but she didn't want to leave him any opening to attack again. When she looked back at his face, she couldn't even fathom his response.

A *smile.* A big, fat, totally unaffected smile. "All *right,* all right," he conceded with a disgusting giggle as he lowered his hands and shrugged. "You win, okay? Just relax."

He turned around and began to saunter slowly back toward the door. He stopped short at the doorway.

"Get out!" she growled again, walking toward him with the knife. *"Now!"*

"Okay, *okay,*" he said. "I'm just getting my tools. Jesus."

He leaned down and swiped up the lock pick from the floor. The next thing she knew, it was flying from his hand. And flying at her face.

She ducked reflexively, but the moment she faltered, she felt his shoulder slam into her gut, knocking her entire body off the ground as the base of her spine landed with an agonizing thud against the floor. He'd tackled her so fast that she'd completely lost her orientation. There was nothing but a blur of pain and jabs to her hands and face, and suddenly he was on top of her. He was crushing her to the floor with all his weight, straddling his legs over her arms and waist, making it impossible to move. His left hand was wrapped around her neck, holding her head against the floor, and his right hand. . . was now holding the knife.

Tatiana had played it wrong, and she knew it. The fight for her life was over. And he had won.

"Stab me in the *heart?*" he spat. "You were going to stab me in the heart?" He reached back and smacked her face with the back of his hand. She could barely even feel the sting. Because she knew now. She knew that her mother was dead. And Tom was dead, too. Loki was killing them all one by one, and she was next in line. All she had left to hope for was that she'd see her mother on the other side.

"If that's how you like it, that's fine with me," he said. He ran the knife along her throat and placed the point over her heart, smiling at her. "Good night."

Tatiana closed her eyes as tightly as she could and tried to picture her mother. She heard him scream out one last time, and then there was silence.

No one understands it. None of the doctors has a clue. They say there's "no visible retinal damage, no visible nerve damage." They just keep asking me the same questions over and over, and I keep giving them the same answers even though things don't make so much sense in my head right now. I tell them that the police showed up at the apartment and Ed told them to call an ambulance. I tell them that everything just kept getting a little darker while Ed held me.

Ed held me. I love that Ed held me. While we were waiting for the ambulance. As they got me onto the stretcher. As we drove to the hospital.

Darker and darker. Until there was nothing. Just black. Pitch black.

At first I thought I had fainted. Maybe even died. They say that after you die, you can see your body lying there as your soul floats upward. You can still see all the doctors and EMS people

working on you, trying to bring
you back. I thought that would
explain what was going on.

Only I *couldn't* see myself.
And I couldn't see the men in the
ambulance, either. I could only
hear them. I kept asking them
what was happening to me. I kept
screaming out that question over
and over like some horrific broken record. "What's happening to
me?" And they just kept yelling
at me, ordering me to follow
their fingers with my eyes,
ordering me to look wherever they
were snapping. And I told them I
couldn't. I told them a hundred
times that I couldn't see.

I can't see anything. And they
have no idea why.

Of course, I couldn't tell
them everything. Then they would
think I was blind *and* crazy. I
couldn't tell them about the drug
Josh gave me, about Gaia's uncle,
about being fearless for a few
days and then losing my freaking
mind. So much of it is a blur,
anyway. I mean, I've completely

lost track of *what* happened *when*.
I remember Josh being with me,
trying to give me another drug,
maybe? The antidote to the drug
that ruined me? I'm not sure. And
then he was gone, and then. . . I
think he was there again. . . or
maybe that was the time before.
Sometimes everything makes sense,
and then it gets cloudy again. I
don't know. . . .

I know that I'm getting sicker.
My brain is getting sicker.
That's why I don't know things.
That's why I don't remember
things. I know it. The doctors
know it, too. My body is shutting
down. I can feel it. I think
maybe I'm dying. I mean. . . I
know I am. But no one knows why.

Except I know why. I do.

I'm being punished, that's why.
My going blind is some kind of
punishment from God.

It's just like that play we
read in class. *Oedipus Rex*.
Oedipus was this king who thought
he could find some way to cheat
his own destiny. He thought he

could outsmart the gods. Like he was above the gods or something. Like he was above *everyone*. It's called *hubris.*

And that's me. That's been me my whole life. Acting like some kind of queen, placing myself so far above everyone and every-thing. It's like, no matter who is in the room, I have to figure out why I'm above them in some way or else. . . or else I'm not me. Or else who am I? Like I'm no one if I'm not better than someone else. I wish I knew if I was mak-ing sense. It's not coming out right, but it's making so much sense now in my head.

That's what I tried to do to Gaia when I took that fearless drug. I wanted to beat her at her own game. I wanted to. . . I don't know. . . *conquer* her, prove that I was above her. And I think maybe that was the last straw. God knew I was trying to cheat with that drug, and he decided that it was finally time to punish me for all my stupid pride once and for all—to punish me for my hubris.

When Oedipus realized all the awful things he had done, he got so disgusted and ashamed of himself that he actually gouged out his own eyes. The blindness was like a part of his punishment. And now it's mine. That's the whole irony of this thing. It took my going blind to finally see everything clearly—to finally see how all my stupid pride has screwed me.

But I get it now. I finally get it. My life is not a goddamned contest. There's no "big winner" at the end. There's no prize. I'm no better than anyone else. And that includes Gaia Moore. I get it now. I get it just in time to die.

God, I'm scared. The drug. . . It still does weird things to my head. I can feel it. I'm so scared for the rest of it to go black—my hearing and then my mind. I need to tell everyone what I've learned. I need to make up for what I've done. Maybe then

the gods will. . . you know. . .
forgive me. Maybe. I need to tell
Gaia. I need to tell Ed and Josh.
   Josh. What happened to Josh?
Where is he? Why hasn't he come
to see me in the hospital?
Unless. . . oh God. . .
   Maybe the gods have punished
him, too.

AT SOME POINT GAIA STOPPED LISTENING

to Heather. Probably around the time she had started to picture the two of them in cages. Heather and her in metal cages, smacking a giant lever for food pellets, sucking at a giant bottle on the wall for water, one drop

Blind Optimism

at a time. Running in their giant metal wheels. Waiting for the occasional carrot stick. . .

Human guinea pigs. That's all they were to Loki. Fat little balls of matted fur with black vacant eyes and brains the size of a pea. Nothing but disposable lab rats.

If he didn't die for any of his other long list of sick atrocities, he had to die for what he had done to Heather Gannis. Blind. The bastard had made her blind. A girl who had absolutely *nothing* to do with *anything*. A girl who was barely even Gaia's *friend*. Gaia had always thought there were certain limits to Loki's maniacal tendencies. But clearly his boundaries were long gone. People were no longer people to him. They were just test samples—masses of tissue and blood and genetic code. He probably had a stack of human test subjects frozen in some locker somewhere, like frogs waiting to be dissected by a room full of squeamish sixth graders.

He can't be my father. He cannot be my father. . . .

Heather had asked her family to leave the room, which, Gaia was ashamed to say, was a gargantuan relief. But once Gaia, Heather, and Ed were alone in the room, Heather began to speak. And once she had opened her mouth, Gaia's relief disappeared in a puff of horrifying black smoke.

Heather was still talking a mile a minute, sometimes only half making sense, but she'd already told Gaia enough. She'd told her about the drug that was supposed to make her fearless like Gaia and about all the other promises Loki and Josh had made. She'd told her about all the horrific side effects—the body tremors, the uncontrollable shouts and violent fits, finally explaining Heather's bizarre behavior of the last few days. And, of course, all the other horrible side effects that had brought her here to the hospital: the confusion, the incapacitating sickness, and now her loss of sight. And she'd confessed every word of it right in front of Ed Fargo.

Gaia and Ed were seated on either side of Heather's bed, face-to-face. Or rather, they would have been face-to-face if Gaia had been able to look at him. But it was hard enough for her to face Heather's ordeal, let alone take on the thousand unspoken feelings hovering between her and Ed. She had still only looked him in the eye a total of about four times since walking into this room.

Allowing him to hear all of this was only making Gaia more uncomfortable. It could only be dangerous for him to hear the real extent of Loki's evil. But Gaia couldn't have shut Heather up if she'd tried. Heather needed to tell her story. It was almost like the emotional equivalent of having her stomach pumped. Like if she didn't puke all the facts out right now, then she just might die from keeping them in her system. Although, God help her, Gaia wasn't sure Heather was going to live regardless. Her breaths were so shallow, her skin so jaundiced. Occasionally her limbs would break into mild, involuntary tremors. Occasionally she would talk in nothing but gibberish. She'd already lost her sight and some degree of brain function. Gaia was dreading what she might lose next.

"I'm fool," Heather uttered incoherently, gazing blankly at the ceiling. "No, I'm *a* fool. I am so sorry. I didn't know what I was doing. Say you forgive me, Gaia. Please say you forgive me...."

Heather reached to her right, grasping to find Gaia's hand. Gaia quickly took hold and leaned in closer. She still couldn't believe after her whole "pilgrimage of guilt" from her house to the hospital that Heather was lying there asking *Gaia* to forgive *her*.

"It's *okay*," Gaia said, squeezing Heather's fragile hand. "You don't need to apologize. This wasn't your fault. This was *them. They* did this."

"I wanted to hurt you," Heather admitted as tears began to fall from her eyes again.

"It's okay, Heather," Ed assured her.

"I don't care," Gaia promised her. "You only felt that way because Loki was screwing with your head and Josh was manipulating the crap out of you—"

"*No,*" Heather interrupted, shaking her head wildly from side to side. "Not Josh. Josh loved me. Josh wanted to fix me, but I wouldn't let him."

Gaia dropped her head in anger. The son of a bitch had Heather completely snowed. He actually had her convinced that he loved her. How could Gaia possibly get it through Heather's sick and foggy head that Josh felt anything *but* love for her? That he couldn't care less if she dropped dead at this very moment, lying between Gaia and Ed in a sweat-stained hospital bed with her parents praying for her out in the hall? *Fix her?* What the hell did that mean?

"Heather. What do you mean, Josh wanted to 'fix you'?"

"Something counter," Heather mumbled, licking under her lips to fight off her dry mouth and then swallowing slowly.

"What?"

"Counter. . . ," she uttered again, making absolutely no sense. "Counter. . ." She blinked down hard over her vacant eyes with frustration. "*Counteragent.* Josh tried to give me the *counteragent* to the drug. Because he loves me, Gaia. But I wouldn't let him. . . ."

"Wait, there's a counteragent?" Gaia asked urgently.

"Yes. I don't know."

"Yes or *no?*" Gaia felt herself giving in to frustration again. How the hell was she supposed to know if anything Heather was saying was true or not? If there was an antidote to the drug that had poisoned Heather—if there was *any* way for there to be one less casualty in this disgusting war, Gaia needed to know about it. But with Heather in this state, there was no way to know anything for sure, and Gaia was losing patience fast. "Heather. Is there a counteragent or *not? Yes* or *no?*"

"Gaia, come on," Ed said, scolding her with his eyes.

"Don't yell, Gaia, *please,*" Heather whimpered. "You hate me. I know you hate me."

"No," Gaia insisted, looking to Ed for forgiveness as she spoke to Heather. "I'm sorry. I didn't mean to yell, Heather. I just want to help you. I didn't—"

"You despise me," she cried. "I know you do."

"*No,*" Gaia insisted. "That's not true, Heather. All I'm trying to do is—"

"I just wanted to be like *you,* Gaia!"

This sudden outburst stunned Gaia and Ed into complete silence.

Gaia stared at Heather's stricken expression. Now she was quite sure that Heather had lost her mind. Either that or she was just speaking nonsensical gibberish again. Because no one. . . *no one* in their right mind could possibly want to be like Gaia. Especially someone like Heather Gannis—someone that sane people actually did want to be like.

"That's why I did it," Heather went on, closing her eyes as she spoke. For a moment she suddenly seemed completely lucid. "That's why I took that drug. I just. . . I wanted your strength. I wanted to be stronger than you. No, I wanted to be *you*, but stronger. No, that's not even it. I mean, yes, I wanted to know what it felt like to be empowered like you, but. . . that's not why I took the drug, Gaia. That's not why I wanted to be like you. Oh God, what am I babbling for—it's *obvious*, isn't it? I just. . . I just wanted them to love me the way they love you. The way Sam loved you. The way Ed loves you." Heather opened her eyes and gazed up at some unknowable image in her head. "I wanted Ed to look at me the way he looks at you. The way he's probably looking at you right now."

Gaia's eyes drifted toward Ed. Heather had either momentarily regained her sight or else she was psychic. Because Ed *was* looking at Gaia. And while she couldn't possibly define what his look meant, she could feel his dark brown eyes tugging her forward and nearly pulling her to him across the bed. . . .

They both turned away. Gaia could only assume that Ed had turned away for the same reason she had. The shame of being caught by a girl who couldn't even see.

That's what was so shameful about this feeling for Ed. She couldn't control it. And that's what was going to get Ed killed if she didn't do something about it. Gaia had tried everything to sever ties with Ed. She'd avoided him, she'd insulted him, she'd told him all kinds of cruel lies. But she could do nothing to curb her feelings, regardless of all the grave, tragic circumstances that surely should have taken precedent. People were dying. Loki was roaming around out there somewhere, drugging people, putting innocent people in the hospital, setting buildings on fire. Heather was lying right between them, suffering, and still. . . one look in Ed's eyes and it all fell away.

Maybe that was the real reason she'd worked so hard to avoid eye contact tonight. Because two uninterrupted seconds in Ed's eyes and Gaia was right back in bed with him, wrapped up in his purple sheets, rolling around in blind optimism while the rest of the world was falling apart. And she couldn't let that happen again. She would never again be caught indulging in some foolish romantic fantasy about Ed while his potential murderer snuck up from behind. She had to keep her eyes wide open. And she couldn't do that if she was gazing at Ed.

"What's going *on* in here?" Heather's mother was suddenly standing in the doorway, looking possessed. Before Gaia could even open her mouth, Mrs. Gannis had all but hip-checked Gaia out of the way to tend to Heather. "Why is she crying? Why is my daughter crying?" She turned around and gave Gaia a primitive death glare. "What did you do? What did you say to her?"

Gaia suddenly felt the irrational

need to find a hole and crawl inside.

"No, no." Ed stood up out of his chair. "Mrs. Gannis, it's nothing like that. We were just—"

"Mom, cut it *out*," Heather demanded. "You don't know what you're saying! Gaia didn't do a thing wrong. She's not... she's not... not me. I'm her. Not me..."

Heather was beginning to fade again. Her moment of lucidity had clearly passed. She whispered a few more incoherent words as her father and sister entered the room.

"What, sweetheart?" Mrs. Gannis asked desperately, leaning her ear as close to Heather's lips as she could manage. "What are you saying?"

But everyone in the room knew what she was saying. Everyone but Mrs. Gannis, whose denial made Gaia feel like crying again.

Heather was saying absolutely nothing. Of course, in her own head she was probably saying a great deal, but all that was coming out was gibberish. Half words and faint, exhausted whimpers.

Mrs. Gannis stepped away from the bed and turned back to Ed and Gaia. Her face had gone completely cold. "Visiting hours are over," she stated definitively. "I think you should go... both of you. I'd like to say good night to my daughter. Without you here."

"Sure," Ed said, trying in vain to make the moment seem normal. "We'll get going. Heather, I'll call you, okay?"

Heather was still mumbling to herself in her own world.

Ed walked to the door and opened it. "Gaia. . . ? You coming?"

"Yeah," Gaia replied, trying to unglue her eyes from Heather's pale gray face. "Heather, I'll. . . I'll come back, okay? I'll—"

"Good night," Mrs. Gannis interrupted, tacking on a horrid fake smile just to push Gaia along.

"Good night," Gaia muttered as she backed away to the door. "You're safe, okay? You're going to be fine here with your family, so don't worry now, and. . . just get some rest, and—"

"*Gaia,*" Ed cut her off, subtly indicating Mrs. Gannis's stern expression, belying her desperate desire for Gaia to get the hell out of that room.

"Okay," Gaia breathed. Standing right by Ed at the door, she realized just how utterly twisted her world had become.

She was stalling. She did not want to leave Heather's side. Gaia Moore did not want to leave Heather Gannis's side. This truly was the twilight zone.

But she finally gave up and turned around, following Ed out of the room. After all, there was really nothing else she could say. She'd already resorted to telling Heather lies. *You don't have to worry now? You're safe?* Those were big, fat, monstrous, supersize lies.

With the exception of telling Ed that she didn't love him, they were probably the biggest lies Gaia had ever told. Now that she'd heard Heather's entire story, she knew the truth.

They were all far from safe. And there was plenty to worry about. So much more than Gaia had even imagined.

ALL TOM HAD SEEN WAS THE KNIFE.

Autopilot

One glimpse of that faint glint of light reflecting off that shiny, jagged blade and he had launched off of his scraped-up, aching, exhausted feet and aimed for the bastard's wrist.

There had been no time to consider the absolute absurdity of it. No time to wonder how he could possibly be opening his own front door on another deadly crisis—another millisecond between life and death after the entire harrowing nightmare he and Natasha had just returned from in the Caymans.

They'd finally found their way home from Loki's endless succession of horrors and death traps, and all Tom had wanted to do when he'd opened that door was to sit in a chair for at least three legitimately calm minutes. Just three minutes before he voluntarily reentered

61

hell. Three minutes of holding his beautiful daughter. Three minutes of sitting at a simple wooden dining table with Natasha instead of in a torture chamber or a prison cell or even a turbulent flight back to the States. Three minutes to take a look around that table and see the woman he'd fallen in love with safe at home and her daughter and his daughter seated together like sisters. A family. That's what they could have and *should* have been building right there in that house. That's what he had so hoped to come home to. An honest-to-goodness family. But that was utterly impossible as long as one particular family member continued to breathe.

Tom had honestly thought he might have found three decent minutes to dream about a new future instead of obsessing over his deadly and tiresome past, but one glimpse of that knife and he knew. . . .

To expect three minutes of his life without Loki was to expect too much.

So there had been no time to wonder whether or not his lifesaving reflexes would kick in. The fact was, they already had. Tom was on lifesaving autopilot at this point. As was Natasha. So neither one of them had thought twice when they opened the door and saw a man in black crushing one of their daughters to the floor and raising a knife in the air for a quick and brutal kill. They had simply reacted.

Tom took to the air and aimed for the knife, terrified

to even know who he was trying to save. Was it Gaia trapped under the man's legs? Was it Tatiana? If Tom and Natasha had opened that door three seconds later, would they have walked in to find one of their children stabbed to death, lying in a pool of blood with a knife through her chest? It was nothing short of a miracle that they'd walked in when they had. But that made sense, Tom supposed. He knew that it would take more than a few miracles to defeat Loki. He'd realized that years ago.

He rushed forward and grabbed onto the man's wrist from behind, knocking the knife from his hand and ramming his shoulder straight into the center of the man's spine, forcing an excruciating howl out of him as he knocked him against some object he couldn't see and rolled him flat against the floor.

Natasha ran in right behind Tom and jumped down to the girl's side. Tom shot a glance at to Natasha and saw her shoulders slump forward. He couldn't even tell if her gesture had been one of relief or anguish. He looked down to the girl's face, and he realized. . . it was Tatiana he had saved, not Gaia. "Is she all right?" Tom called to Natasha, grabbing onto the assailant's wrist and twisting his arm painfully behind his back.

Natasha didn't waste a moment. She frisked her daughter for potential injuries and then pressed her fingers to her neck. "No wounds," she announced, sounding on the verge of tears as the words fell quickly from her lips. "She's *alive*, Tom. She's out cold, but she is definitely alive."

Tom breathed an internal sigh of tremendous relief. He immediately understood what must have happened. The mystery object that the man had hit wasn't an object at all. It was Tatiana's head. That was why she was out cold. The bastard's knee must have smacked straight into her chin as Tom tackled him off her. Out cold but alive. *Miracle number two.*

Tom turned back to Loki's hired dummy and drove his face into the cold wood floor. "You hear that, you son of a bitch? She's alive. You screwed it up. You know what Loki does to people who screw things up? It's a hell of a lot worse than what you were going to do to her. I can't wait to—"

Tom should have known better than to gloat. It wasn't even like him. He was just so utterly at his wits' end with Loki and every one of his brainless, spineless, reptilian henchmen. But one tiny moment of hubris and he hadn't seen the punch coming. Or was it a kick?

Somehow the hooded thug had managed to twist his entire body over and kick Tom in the face, whipping his head against the corner of the dining table. The sting was like nothing Tom had encountered in years of service to his country.

"Tom?" Natasha shouted. "Are you all right?"

A vicious wave of vertigo crashed over Tom's head, spinning the entire room into circles within circles. He clutched at his wound and tried to shake out the roller-coaster ride in his brain. "I can't quite. . ."

The man in black took this chance to leap up from the floor and slip away from Tom. Tom swiped out his arm to catch the thug, but he missed by a mile, still trying to get his bearings straight. He could see Natasha rising to her feet through his wavy fish-tank vision. She whipped her gun out from inside her coat.

"*Freeze*," she hollered, double gripping the gun and thrusting her arms forward. But the thug was no slug. Not by a long shot. Tom watched in utter shock as he leapt high up into the air and snapped his leg forward with a pinpoint flying kick straight into Natasha's face. The gun flew from her hands as she went rocketing backward, falling headfirst into a coffee table and shattering every glass- and porcelain-framed picture on the table.

Tom snapped to attention instantly, jumping to his feet. Dizziness gone. Confusion gone. There was no way one of Loki's pathetic clansmen was going to overpower two of the CIA's top agents. He clamped his hand around his gun and whipped it forward, targeting the man's shoulder to put him out of commission so he could cuff him for questioning. But the thug was moving too fast.

Tom squeezed off three quick shots, but the man had already leapt and rolled under the dining table. Tom dropped to one knee and tried to spot him under the table, but he was already moving again. He shot out from under the table and rolled for the dark hall-way that led to the bedrooms.

"You okay?" Tom double-checked with Natasha as he started for the hallway.

"I'm *fine*," she announced, clearly furious with herself for letting her daughter's attempted murderer take her down and get away.

Get used to it, Natasha, Tom thought. *Trust me, I know the feeling, and it doesn't get any better. You just have to get back up and fight him. Again, and again, and again. . .*

Natasha made a move for the hallway, but Tom shook her out of her rash need for instant vengeance. "No, stay here," he insisted. "You stay here and protect your daughter. I've got him."

Stay here and protect your daughter. Such simple advice. Such an obvious prescription for safety. Why was it so easy to see when it was someone *else?* When the hell was Tom going to come to his senses and take his own advice? Stop falling into every one of Loki's wild-goose chases and just stick by his daughter at all times?

This time it will be different, he swore to himself as he streaked down the hall. *This time I'm going to stick by Gaia and never leave her side again. That is that.*

But that thought only led to a far more pressing question he hadn't yet considered in all the chaos. *Gaia.* Where the hell was Gaia?

All these
days of
zombifying
self-enforced
deprivation, **those**
and here
purple
at last
was a
sheets
moment of
critical
relief.

The last two years have made me despise hospitals. I mean, I'm sure everyone despises hospitals, but I doubt they had to go through what I did every time I set foot in St. Vincent's. So to speak.

Three words: *monthly spinal tap.*

Monthly. I know of no pain equal to that of a spinal tap. . . because there is none. Honestly, it had reached the point where all I had to do was come near a hospital hallway and my back and limbs would literally start to throb with pain. It was the ultimate in behavior modification. I never wanted to go within thirty yards of another medical institution. That's why I insisted on doing most of my physical therapy at home. Anything to avoid another trip to the hospital.

But that all changed today. As of today, I have hereby established an overwhelming affinity for hospitals. I honestly felt like kissing the walls of St. Vincent's, and I don't really care how sick that sounds. Because today, something damn near glorious occurred in that pasty and depressing white room. And yes, a part of me feels guilty as all hell for saying that, given the nightmare Heather has been through. But the glorious might never have happened otherwise. Heather would never have been so completely honest if it weren't for what she'd been through, and then she never would have brought everything out in the open.

Maybe all those butt-annoying people who used to tell me that "something good always comes from a tragedy" weren't as full of crap as I thought they were. I mean, now that I'm walking again, I can guarantee those people that walking beats the chair, hands down, but still, I guess sometimes it takes a tragedy for something to change for the better. Sometimes it takes a tragedy for the truth to come out.

Today, sitting across from Gaia in that hospital room, I

finally saw the truth. I saw it in her eyes. And I heard it in Heather's story. I *felt* it.

Gaia is still in love with me. She still loves me. She never stopped loving me.

This whole treating-me-like-a-plague thing. . . is all about her uncle. I know it now. After hearing everything Heather had to say and watching the way Gaia looked at me, I'm positive. She's just being *Gaia*. She's playing the goddamned hero again. She's been staying away from me to protect me from him, not because she hates my guts, but because they are going after anyone who's even remotely close to her.

I bet Gaia's uncle was behind my shooting, too. He's obviously capable of a hell of a lot worse. He was probably the one who sent that gun-toting asshole after me. *Of course*. That makes perfect sense. That's when Gaia turned on me, right out of the freaking clear blue sky. Right after she'd seen me get shot at. No, I should rephrase that.

Right after her uncle tried to kill me.

And that's when I lost her.

Who *is* this guy? Gaia's uncle. Why is he such a sick bastard? What the hell happened to him as a kid? And why hasn't the son of a bitch been locked up or just plain *put down?* After what he's done to Gaia, and to Sam, and to Heather, and to *me*, for Christ's sake. Why don't they just put him out of his misery? That's obviously the only way anyone is ever going to stop him.

I should have done it. I should have just ripped into him that day I watched him sniffing around school for Gaia. I could have ended it right there, and then Heather would have been absolutely fine and Gaia and I would *still* probably be in bed. If I ever get the chance again. . . I swear to God, if I ever see him again, I'm not going to hesitate. I don't know what I'll do to him, but I guarantee he won't be standing when I'm done.

But I'll have to deal with that *then*. And I'll be back to visit Heather in the hospital tomorrow and every day after that. And I'll do whatever I can for her, whenever she needs it. But right now. . . Right at this very moment, I'm not thinking about tomorrow or the next day. Right now, all I'm thinking about is Gaia's gorgeous profile set against the ugly white walls of a hospital hallway. And what a complete idiot I've been. I was right not to trust her freakish change of heart in the first place. The world *isn't* that cruel. People *can't* fall out of love with you in fifteen minutes.

It's really no different than what happened with my legs. Here I was walking around on crutches for I don't even know how many extra days, maybe even weeks, thinking I couldn't use my legs. Like I was glued to the ground without my crutches or something. But it turned out I wasn't really glued to the ground at all. My legs were just standing there, waiting for me to fix my screwed-up head, waiting for me to dump all my subconscious fears and take control. And it's the same with Gaia. I've been sitting here moping around, believing all the fearful voices in my head telling me I'd lost her, telling me I'd never even had her in the first place. But the truth is, she's been there the whole time. I just need to dump my fears and go back to my instincts. That's what I have to do.

Because if there's one thing I've learned after two years in that chair and watching Heather laid out on that hospital bed, it's that there is no time in this life to listen to those fearful voices. I need to move forward, and Gaia is coming with me. I will not stay glued to the ground. That is not going to happen.

HE'D NEVER QUITE BEEN ABLE TO

figure out how she did it. All that bitterness and distrust and sorrow should have made her so ugly, shouldn't it? Wasn't inner joy and inner peace what made people beautiful? That angelic glow that always shone through in old masters' paintings and old Hollywood movies? Wasn't that beauty? Yes, in every other case but this one. But that made sense, Ed supposed. Gaia was an exception to just about every rule. Here she was, set against the dank halls of a hospital, her tangled hair falling down her shoulders in greasy tendrils, staring straight ahead with a cold, vengeful glare, looking so pale and exhausted under the gray-blue fluorescent light. . .

And she was beautiful.

More than beautiful. Something about her transcended the entire scene. She wasn't like those paintings of docile angelic maidens with their cherubic inner glow. No, she was like the paintings of the martyrs and the warriors. Joan of Arc. The steely-eyed Greek goddesses on bucking horses with swords over their heads, forging on through a sea of enemies, weathering the winds of Zeus or whatever the hell else got in their way. That was Gaia. A warrior goddess, forging on through the crap-storm of her life, yet somehow always seeming completely untouched by the crap.

Ed tried to keep pace with her as they sped down the only available hallways. One of the beauties of walking was that Ed could finally keep up with Gaia's determined stomping without getting tire burns from pumping his wheels or underarm cramps from pumping his crutches. He matched her step for step, and with each overdriven stride, he struggled to find the right first words. He had to find the words that would cut through her lies and bring her back. "Look, I—"

"Now's not a good time to talk, Ed," she snapped coldly, keeping her eyes fixed straight ahead as they made their way down a particularly long hall.

"Gaia, come on, can we just—"

"*Ed.*" Gaia swiveled her head to all sides, darting her eyes suspiciously through every doorway they passed. She was obviously convinced that her uncle could be waiting around any corner at any time. Her uncle probably *was* waiting just inside the next room down the hall, holding his finger to the trigger of an AK-47 and counting down from three. But that possibility was not going to hold Ed back at this point. And not for any good reason. It wasn't as if he were being particularly brave. In fact, he was quite sure he was indulging in new heights of stupidity. But when you realize that you *haven't* lost the love of your life after days and days of head-crushing depression, you'll do incredibly stupid things. And you won't care.

At this point, Ed was basically applying skaters' law to matters of the heart. Rule number five in Shred's Personal Skating Manifesto: If you see a great jump, you must take it. You can figure out the landing later.

"You know. . . I can take care of myself," he offered tentatively.

"Glad to hear it," she muttered in response.

"I mean, if, for instance, maybe you were treating me like crap to keep me away from you. . . so that you could *protect* me, you know, from your uncle. . ." He checked for a reaction and got absolutely nothing. He couldn't even get her eyes to roll in his direction. "Well, that wouldn't be necessary," he said. "I mean, I appreciate the thought, but it's not necessary."

"That's not what's going on," she assured him quickly, sounding almost too insistent. Her head dropped so that she was staring at the floor. And she began to pick up the pace. "And even if it *were,* you wouldn't have any clue what was necessary. In case you hadn't noticed, Heather is *dying* in there, so I'd cut the whole I-can-take-care-of-myself routine. When it comes to my uncle, no one can take care of a goddamn thing."

"I know that. I'm just trying to say that you are not responsible for everything that happens to everybody—"

"Yes, I *am,* Ed." She halted suddenly, turning just to assault Ed with those warrior eyes. "I *am* responsible. I am responsible for all of this. All of it."

Her guilty eyes left Ed momentarily speechless. He wasn't even sure why. It could have been the anger, or the beauty, or just one empathic moment of feeling how heavy a burden she'd been carrying all this time. Whatever it was, it made his heart hurt for a moment. And Gaia used that moment to take off at an even brisker stomping speed.

Ed quickly shook off his freeze-up and chased her down. He had to be quick because they had finally come upon a hallway with an exit on either end, and he knew that she would take whichever route he didn't. And then he'd lose the moment. And then he would have to try to create another moment, and with Gaia's unparalleled avoidance skills, that moment might not present itself for another five years.

Don't listen to her, Ed. That's the trick. And for God's sake, don't listen to yourself, either. Just do what's real. This thing she's doing, this is all smoke and mirrors. Just cut to the real part. Cut to the truth. And do it now, you idiot. She's three steps from good-bye.

"I'll talk to you later, okay?" Gaia's back was already to Ed as she turned the corner toward the exit.

"Gaia, *wait.*" Ed reached out and grasped her arm. The sudden shift in momentum spun her back toward him before she could pull away. For one sweet moment their faces were only an inch apart, but Gaia quickly regained her balance and took a step back. Though she didn't yank her arm from his grip.

"What?" she asked impatiently.

"J-Just. . . ," Ed stammered. It wasn't as if he'd prepared his remarks here. "Just let me. . ."

Gaia began to pull her arm away. Her eyes were darting around to all sides again, scanning the halls suspiciously, like some cyborg scanning for the enemy. "Ed, I'm going home, and I want you to go home, okay? Get off me and go *home.*"

"No, I need to. . ." Again he had nothing. No more words. *Three seconds, Ed. Three more seconds of this wimpy crap and she's gone.* How was he supposed to talk to her when she kept shifting her watchful eyes in all directions, like some paranoid soldier?

"Ed, let go, okay? Just let go." She pulled her arm away.

"This is ridiculous!" Ed blurted. "I can't talk to you like this." He turned behind him and saw the door to a janitor's closet. *Fine. Good. No more hesitation. Go.*

He clasped her hand tightly and tugged. "In here. They can't *see* us in here." He threw open the door and pulled Gaia into the cramped quarters of the janitor's closet, moving so swiftly that Gaia couldn't resist. Or maybe, just *maybe,* some part of her didn't want to resist. Whatever the reason, and however loudly she huffed with frustration and dismay, she stepped in after him. And before she could possibly change her mind, Ed slammed the door behind her, stepping so close to her that she was forced to push her back against the door just to keep her distance from him.

But there was no room for distance. However much Gaia might have wished for it, distance was no longer an option. There was, in fact, so little room to stand that Ed was forced to lean his hands against the door on either side of her face, holding his arms extended just to keep from falling against her. And now Ed was sure that there was such a thing as fate. Because fate had put a six-by-six janitor's closet between the last hallway and the last exit on this floor. Fate had placed them in the right proximity for an honest conversation.

Finally they were close. Close like they were supposed to be. Close enough to hear each other breathing in the sudden quiet. Close enough to push their overly active brains out of the equation.

There was the faintest bit of dim yellow light coming from a dying bulb in a gray metal casing on the ceiling. Just enough light to bring the cluttered steel shelves surrounding them out of the shadow. Just enough light to see the mop and two rolling buckets on the floor that left them nowhere else to step. And just enough light to trace her eyes and her nose and the perfect outline of her mouth.

"Ed," she complained. Her voice sounded tight and strained. She kept her arms glued against the door.

"Shhh." Ed placed his finger against his lips. "If

you're that worried about them seeing us, I know you don't want them to hear us, either."

"I don't know what you're talking about," she whispered harshly. "Ed, I can't stay in here."

"Gaia, can we just tell the truth in here? Let's stick with the truth."

"What the hell are you talking about? Who's lying?"

"God, I can't believe this. I can't believe *you're* the one who's scared here. Does that make any sense? That makes no sense. If your uncle's coming after everyone you know, shouldn't *I* be the one freaking out right now? But I'm not, Gaia. I'm not scared of him. Jesus, the psycho has already tried to blow holes in my head, and I'm still not scared. And I have *no* idea why I'm not scared, but honestly, right now I'm much more freaked out by the fact that you are."

"I am *not* scared," she insisted, raising her volume above a whisper as she pummeled him with her eyes. "I just don't want to be cramped in a freaking janitor's closet with you. Fear's got nothing to do with it. I already told you, we can't be this close. I don't want to be this close to you—"

"Gaia, stop it," Ed whispered, leaning his face even closer just to shut her up. "You don't need to do this anymore. You don't need to lie to protect me. I *know*."

"Know *what*?" Gaia scoffed.

"I *know*. I know what I heard in there. I know what

I saw. I know what your uncle is capable of. I know what he's trying to do. I know he tried to kill me once and he'll probably try again. But more important than that, I know what I saw when you looked at me in that room.

"This is all a load of crap you're giving me—this attitude, this avoiding-me-like-the-plague thing, it's a lie. And it started the moment you saw me get shot at. You don't hate my guts. What we did together wasn't a *mistake*. You love me, Gaia. You love me just as much as I love you. So why don't you stop going for the Oscar here and admit it so I can stop leaning against this goddamned door and touch you."

Gaia huffed out a loud, disgusted grunt and crossed her arms firmly. "You presumptuous freak!"

"Shhhhh," Ed warned.

"You presumptuous freak," she whispered. "You don't know what you're talking about. I'm. . . I'm sorry to interfere with your delusions, but. . . but this has *nothing* to do with my uncle. I just can't be with you like that, okay?"

"Gaia, you're not hearing me. I know you're lying. Don't ask me why I'm so sure—I just am. I know you still love me. And I know what you're trying to do, but I'm telling you, it's a mistake."

"Please, just—," Gaia started.

But Ed wouldn't let her speak. "No one is safe *either way*, don't you get it? It doesn't matter if he sees us together or not. Look at Heather. Either he gets us or he doesn't. That's true whether you and I are together or not. And if you keep pulling this crap with me, then we're going to end up without a stitch of happiness in this whole scenario."

"Ed—"

"*Gaia,*" he snapped. "Listen to me now. I'm going to let my hands go from this door. I'm going to wrap them around your waist, and I am going to kiss you."

"Ed, goddammit, please just listen—"

"*No.* Listening to you is what messed us up in the first place. We should be holding each other and touching each other and kissing each other. Do you know how many days of the best kissing and touching we've missed here? The *beginning-of-a-relationship* kissing? I mean, *Jesus. No one* has the right to steal that from us. No one."

Ed took a deep breath, swallowed hard, dropped his hands from the door, and wrapped them around Gaia's waist. By now his eyes had adjusted to the dim light, and he was beginning to be able to see Gaia's eyes completely. He could see that at least they were no longer darting from side to side with worry but simply fixed on his.

"Gaia, please," he said quietly. "I don't want to play anymore. I'm all out of psychotic. You have to let me know now. 'Cause the real truth. . . I don't know what the hell I'm talking about here. Maybe you really do hate my guts, and your stalker ex-boyfriend just trapped you in a closet for two minutes, and you'll need years of extensive therapy to recover. If that's true, then I am *so* sorry. But if that's not true... if your entire body is buzzing from being next to me in this closet the way mine is buzzing from finally being this close to you again... then please, please tell me the truth. We can go back out there right now and face all those freaking horrors and death traps alone, or we can stay in here for a few more minutes and... I don't know... just... be together. So just tell me the truth now and I will never ask you again. Do you want to be together? Do you want—"

Gaia shut Ed's mouth with her own. She clasped both her hands firmly around the back of his neck, pressed her lips to his lips, pressed her body to his body, and answered his question, clinging to him so strongly, it was almost as if she were afraid she might lose him again. They fell against the door as he wrapped his arms tightly around her waist, reaching his hands all the way around her back and grabbing onto her. His hands weren't really within his control at this point as they swept forcefully up to her back and then to the back of her head, pressing her to him, breathing her in with the desperation of a man who'd been slowly suffocating for days. And in all honesty, he had been.

GAIA LET HERSELF GIVE IN. SHE

just did. It was entirely beyond her control. And she didn't care. Finally, for at least two whole minutes, she didn't care about all the watchful eyes and impending doom. She didn't

Philosophical Questions

care about her enemies. She didn't care who her father was. She didn't care about what joylessly heroic thing she was supposed to do next. All those things were surely waiting for her down on the ground somewhere. But as long as she had Ed's lips, as long she had his body pressing her against that door, she could hover just slightly above all of it, feeling weightless and resurrected in this cold cement janitor's closet.

Resurrected. That was honestly the feeling coursing through her veins. Being brought back from the dead. At least for two minutes. His kiss was just like oxygen, or food, or water. And Gaia had been starving, parched, and holding her breath without him. All these days of zombifying self-enforced deprivation, and here at last was a moment of critical relief.

She knew she had just broken about twenty different promises by kissing him. Promises she'd made to herself, pacts she'd made with her uncle, and her father, and even Satan.

But Ed was just making too much sense. What was

the use of being fearless if she was going to live what basically amounted to a fearful life? Peering around every corner, tiptoeing on Loki's stupid tightrope all day and all night? Denying herself everything and giving him complete control?

No, it wasn't even that. That's not why she was wrapped in Ed's arms. It was nothing that philosophical or profound. It was so much simpler.

It was just wanting him so much. That's all it was. Wanting him so much that it crossed over into that very pesky category of "need." So much that standing next to him in the dark had been screwing up her breathing. So much that the simple act of being tugged into a cold, wet closet felt like some kind of irresistible foreplay.

She'd given it every bit of resistance she had left. She'd lied through her teeth again and again. She'd glued her hands to that door. She'd barked endless orders to her body to stay cold and stiff—to ignore her racing heart. To stop pumping all that blood through her chest and up to her face. To avoid the electrical sparks she felt just from having his hands on either side of her, pressed against that door.

But none of that was going to do any good. Not in a small, dark room alone with him. Not after resisting him for such a painfully long time. Not after everything he'd said in that remarkably insistent, thoroughly desperate, and beautifully Ed-like monologue. It had been worth kissing him just to shut his verbose ass up, but still, every word had rung true. And as per usual, Ed's uncanny ability to speak the truth had pretty much blown her mangled line of thinking to smithereens.

Ed probably didn't even know how right he was. All this time, Gaia had believed that honoring Loki's clear-cut message to stay away from Ed would somehow keep Ed safe. But Loki was obviously way past honoring any deals, and that included an unspoken deal to leave Ed alone. He'd thrown all of his deranged diplomacy out the window and replaced it with nothing but brute violence and terrorism. So if they were in fact headed toward Loki's version of World War III, why the hell was Gaia wasting time denying herself the only truly good thing still standing in the ruins of her war-torn life?

So she pulled Ed closer. As close as she could bring him with his clothes still on. That still wasn't close enough. And two minutes wasn't enough time. Why should she have to stop at two minutes? If she was through lying to Ed, then why in fact would she ever need or want to leave this room again? If Loki was starting World War III right outside that door, then here was the perfect fallout shelter. They could simply stay together in this closet and wait out the war. All they needed were some cans of beans, plenty of bottled water, and a set of those purple sheets.

Right now, she would have settled for just the sheets.

Ed's hands ignored her clothes completely, sliding urgently under her jacket and her T-shirt and caressing her bare skin. His right hand traveled the length of her spine, lifting the back of her shirt with it, until she could feel her naked shoulders pressed against the metal door. His left hand slid down the base of her back and grabbed on firmly to the waistband of her jeans.

Maybe they didn't even need the sheets.

Gaia was so deeply engrosseed with his lips and his palms and his fingertips, she'd barely even noticed her own hands reaching under his long-sleeved shirt and grasping onto his white undershirt, tugging it out from his jeans, hiking both shirts farther and farther up his chest. . . .

And then, almost simultaneously, they let go of each other.

What's wrong with you, Gaia? What about Heather? And Tatiana, and Natasha, and Dad. . .

Ed must have felt it, too. He must have felt just as ridiculously guilty.

All of them suffering, or missing, or mourning. That was the reality outside this closet. That was what mattered right now. That was surely where Gaia and Ed's minds should have been. But standing here with him, the actual universe had fallen so wondrously far away just for a second. They'd flashed back so completely to the last time they'd been this close that they were ready to take things. . . as far as they could go. Here. Now. In a hospital closet. And that, of course, felt beyond wrong. This was not the time. Not here. Not now. No matter how much they wanted it.

"Okay. . . ," Ed uttered between short, shallow breaths, staring down at the floor, "we were just. . . We can't—"

"No," Gaia agreed, staring straight ahead as she tried to catch her breath. "I didn't even realize I was—"

"Me *neither*," Ed agreed. "I mean. . . well. . . maybe I knew I was. . . but not *here*."

"No. Not here," Gaia agreed.

"Okay." Ed slowly began to breathe more regularly.

"Okay," Gaia echoed.

It was official. They could breathe freely. They had made it out of that very sudden and unexpected "situation" without doing anything too shamefully sinful. No, they weren't bad people—they had just found this one bright match-light of relief in all this oppressive darkness, and those little match-lights were getting harder and harder to come by. But it was time to move on to the next moment, and Gaia knew it.

"I think we need to leave this closet," she said.

"Yeah," Ed replied. "Yeah, we need to leave this closet." They didn't budge.

"I don't want to leave this closet," Ed stated plainly.

"Yeah, I'd kind of rather we stay here in the closet," Gaia agreed.

They stood in comfortable silence for a few moments,

catching their breath and enjoying the quiet pause from all the nightmares outside. And with each breath Gaia realized just how deeply relieved she was. Ed had been the only person left in the world with whom she could breathe freely and easily. And she'd been without those breaths for too long.

Ed, being Ed, was the first to speak again.

"So. . . just. . . to be clear here. . ."

Gaia felt her chest tighten. Why did actual words make her feel more naked than. . . well, than actually *being* naked?

"Yeah. . . ?" she asked, trying not to flinch with discomfort.

"That kiss. . . ," he went on. "Does that kiss mean—?"

"Yes," Gaia assured him, fixing her eyes on a bottle of pine cleaning fluid. Why she needed to stay focused on the cleaning fluid when she felt like proposing marriage. . . . That would probably take her years to understand. Thankfully, Ed seemed to be getting better and better at knowing what she was feeling without any assistance from her. No, that still wasn't giving him the credit he deserved. Ed was beginning to know what she was feeling *in spite* of her.

"Yes. . . ," Ed echoed. "So. . . everything I said to you before was right?"

"What is this, debate team?"

"Gaia." Ed grabbed Gaia's shoulders and turned her to him. Face-to-face. No hospital rooms to peek into, no cleaning fluids to stare at. Just his eyes. He obviously wouldn't be satisfied until he got a straight answer. "Everything I said. . . ," he stated quietly. "That night. . . our night. . . that was *not* a mistake. . . ?"

Gaia took a deep breath and forced her eyes to stay firmly fixed to his. "No," she told him, feeling a two-hundred-pound weight fall from her shoulders and crash at her feet. "That was just about the only right choice I've made in the last five years."

Ed hunched forward, dropping his forehead on her shoulder and smiling as he breathed a huge sigh of relief. "I knew I couldn't be completely crazy."

"You're not crazy," she assured him. "You're completely sane, and I, apparently, am still an idiot."

Finally Gaia breathed her very own long sigh of relief. The truth was finally making its way up from her heart, where she'd been burying it for days, and out of her mouth. And this time, she wanted to be sure she didn't do a damn thing to stop it. Heather had already made her confession. It was time for Gaia to make hers. She took Ed's head in both of her hands and zeroed in on his eyes.

"I doubt you'll ever hear me say this again. . . but you're *right*, Ed," she told him. "Everything you said. I've been lying through my teeth to you, and. . . *that* was the mistake. Not our night together. And Ed, I. . ."

No, don't freeze up again. Not now. Come on, Gaia, for God's sake, say it. Three little words and you've said it. . . .

"And I. . . ," she went on hopelessly. "Well, when I

said that I *didn't* love you. . . I was lying." Not exactly the three words she was trying to say. But it was a good start. "Okay?" she asked, hoping her statement would suffice. Hoping he understood, in spite of her pathetically uncomfortable stammering, that her point was that she was done pretending—that they were together now. No matter what happened.

"Okay," Ed said placing his hand on her cheek. He understood. Of course he understood. "I don't. . . *not* love you, too, Gaia," he said, smiling a wide, comfortable smile. He leaned down and kissed her softly. And Gaia kissed him back. And she could have stayed in that kiss for the next. . .

"Okay," she announced, throwing her body back against the door.

"Right," Ed agreed, pulling back as well. *"Sorry.* I'm sorry."

"No, I started it."

"No, I—"

"Okay, here's the thing," Gaia stated. "We really need to leave this closet now, and we need to go home and not get together until tomorrow."

"Yes," Ed agreed, nodding.

"Yes. Because if we don't leave this closet and go our separate ways at least tonight, then we're just going to start kissing again, and Heather's going be down the hall in that room and. . ."

"We'll end up feeling like the scum of the earth—"

"Right."

"Okay," Ed concurred. "I'm going to go home."

"Okay," she said. "I think I'm going to just. . . take a little time in this closet here."

"Okay. . ." Ed stood up straight and placed his hand on the knob. "So. . . no kiss," he confirmed, inches from her face.

"No kiss," she confirmed, willing her hands to her sides.

"Right." Ed quickly cracked open the door and slipped out through the sudden blinding shaft of light. But she could still feel him behind the door. "Gaia. . ."

"Yeah?" she called back.

"We're going to be okay," he said. "Just don't be afraid. I mean, I know you're never afraid, but. . . we're all going to be all right. Okay?"

"Don't worry," she said, "I'm not afraid, Ed. Believe me."

"Good. Bye," he whispered.

"Bye."

She listened to the miraculous sound of Ed's footsteps trailing off into the distance. And then she stood alone in the dark, claustrophobic closet.

You're not afraid, right? she thought irrationally. *You didn't just put Ed in more danger by telling him the truth, did you?* A moment later her head was flooded with philosophical questions about the nature of fear.

No, of course you're not afraid.

Terrified, maybe. But not afraid.

In all the
darkness,
her emotions
had **tremors**
developed a
mind of
their own.

TOM DOUBLED HIS SPEED AS HE

saw the man in black reach the end of the long hallway and duck into the master bedroom. He was about to run out of space in the apartment, and then Tom would have him cornered.

Something Drastic

He jumped into the master bedroom and flipped on the light. He had just enough time to spot the masked man crouched up on the windowsill of one of the oversized windows. That was it. Nowhere else to run.

But an opposing thought had just begun to enter Tom's mind as the man brought back his leg and smashed a huge, jagged hole in the center of the window. The deafening sound of exploding glass filled the room as a rush of cold wind and shattered glass blew up against Tom's face.

Fire escape. He's still got a fire escape.

He must have known. The bastard must have known his escape route the entire time. This little revelation lost Tom the extra millisecond he'd needed. He thrust the gun forward and started firing through the shattered glass, but the masked man had already ducked through the window and out onto the iron platform.

Tom ran to the window and leapt through the jagged hole, looking down through the iron slats for a target, but when he took his next shot, the faint click of the trigger was all he heard.

Empty. Bad timing. Terrible, terrible timing.

He shoved his gun back in its holster and peered over the banister, hoping to spot the masked man in the increasing darkness of the building's back lot. He could hear the urgent tapping of shoes against metal, headed toward the next level down. The man was moving so damned fast. Tom knew he'd never catch him at this rate. He had to do something drastic. Something that could make up for the lost time. . .

A jump. A full one-story jump down to the next landing to cut him off. It was the only choice. But Tom knew he wasn't his daughter. He'd kept himself in top condition, of course. An agent of his caliber had to. But top condition for a man in his forties. . .

No time for doubt. Tom grabbed onto the edge of the fire escape and swung his entire body over the banister in one swift move, feeling the cold wind and the gravity take hold of him and tug him down to the next level. He knew his feet wouldn't hit the platform first. He wasn't going to land on the platform. He was going to *fall* onto it. But if he stayed focused, he would have the perfect thing to break his fall: a man in a black mask who was running way too quickly.

"Oompf."

Tom's body was bombarded from head to toe by every conceivable surface. Cold black iron, muscular flesh, the wool of a sweater, the rock-hard bones of a knee and an elbow. The two rather sizable men had clashed and rolled up against the edge of the fire escape in a painful heap. For all Tom knew, he'd broken both his legs. Pain was spreading out indiscriminately to every one of his appendages. And the man was already slipping out from under him, as though this world-class collision had barely fazed him. He tugged slowly but surely out of Tom's grip, until all Tom had left to hold on to were his clothes. Tom's hands were just about the only things that were fully functioning right now, so he used them to grip the bloody black ski mask and rip it from the man's face before he broke free.

I've seen this face before, Tom realized. The square, chiseled jaw, the spiky jet-black hair, eyes that were so blue, they were almost purple, and that sickening grin— he'd flashed that disgusting smile the moment Tom had gotten the mask off. Tom never forgot a face. Never. That was something of a prerequisite for the Agency. The only problem was... it was the face of a dead man.

Tom flashed back to that nearly fatal evening at Loki's Chelsea loft. The night Gaia had learned of Sam Moon's death. The night Tom's brother had held a gun to his head and nearly pulled the trigger. He distinctly remembered Loki *killing* this man. He remembered him putting a bullet right through the center of his head. So how exactly could he have survived? How was that possible?

"You're getting way too old for this, Tom," the boy said,

flashing his wicked grin. Despite how desperately Tom wanted to punch him in his fatuous face, he couldn't possibly have agreed more. He *was* getting too old for this. He was sick and tired of this game. So sick and so tired...

Tom struggled to peel himself off the cold iron, but his limbs were shot. He slipped back down onto his hands and knees. "You tell Loki, if he wants to kill Tatiana, he'll have to send someone better than you."

"Jesus, you're pathetic," the boy said with a horrid chuckle, watching joyfully as Tom struggled with his throbbing legs. "You think this is some freaking movie of the week? This whole thing is over, Tom. It's *done*. Gaia will be dead by ten o'clock tomorrow morning."

Tom's eyes shot up to meet the boy's. His statement sounded so definitive, so absolute, that Tom couldn't even hide the fact that it had shaken him to the core. "What are you talking about?" he demanded, raiding the youth's vacant eyes for the truth. "Where's Gaia? What has he done with her?"

"It's not what he's done," he replied. "It's what he's *going* to do."

"*Where is she?*" Tom growled.

"Why don't you ask your buddy George?" he said with a grin. "Or no, I have a better idea. Why don't we have another race, Tom? Let's see who gets to her first. No, I'm kidding. I think we know who's going to get to her first."

Tom couldn't take another word of his taunting. He lunged forward for the boy's legs, but with one swift step back, the boy had Tom grabbing at nothing. Tom could only watch through the iron slats of the fire escape as the boy took off down the steps, heading for the back exit of the building.

"Ready, set, go, Tom," his voice echoed through the dark windy lot. "Last one to Gaia is a rotten egg. . . ."

Tom smashed his hand against the cold iron and sat back against the steps to catch his breath. It was too much information. It was too much horrible information. . . yet no information at all. Where was Gaia? What on earth was going to happen tomorrow at ten o' clock? And what did George know about it?

George. . . my oldest "friend" in the world.

Tom winced at his own sarcasm.

You son of a bitch, George. You traitor. You and I need to talk. It's a talk I've been anxiously awaiting ever since I got my first punch in that torture chamber in the Caymans. And you had better have some answers, George. Gaia's life depends on it.

Memo

From: QR2

To: L

1. Difficulties with phase 1 of Operation Clean Slate. Unexpected skill level for T. Not as easy a mark as expected. Have extricated self from situation. Will need backup to complete this step of OCS.

2. Urgent: Enigma and N have resurfaced. Repeat: Enigma and N have resurfaced. Retreat was necessary. Please advise.

LOKI REREAD THE MEMO AT LEAST three times, his frustration increasing with each read. He could not believe that he was *still* dealing with a liv-

Infestation

ing, breathing brother. He could not fathom his organization's pathetic inability to dispose of Tom and Natasha in the Cayman Islands, after all their concerted efforts. And once again he was compelled to take the blame.

The only feasible explanation for Tom's survival in the Caymans was that Loki had not yet injected himself with the phobosan. He simply had not been as enlightened as he was now—still too attached to his ego-induced fears and anxieties. If Tom wasn't gone, that could only be because, on some deep and tragically weak subconscious level, Loki had not been truly ready for him to go. Some useless leftover "inner child" must have been *afraid* to let him go. But that was just fearful emotional trash left over from when they were little children. Now he was more than ready to say good-bye. God knew he was ready now.

And how could he have underestimated Gaia's young accomplice so completely? What match could that Tatiana girl have possibly been for QR2? How had a complete innocent put up a fight against a qualified replicant with Loki's own personal training and Josh Kendall's supremely conditioned physique?

It had to be Tom. Tom and his usual dumb, ignorant luck. Tom and Natasha must have arrived at that apartment just in time and taken on QR2 together. That was the only feasible explanation. *Tom.* Always Tom, `biting pathetic little holes in Loki's progress, like a nagging infestation.` Nothing but a living, breathing obstacle. Year after year, making it his life's goal to keep Loki's happiness to the bare minimum...

Loki's clenched fist suddenly came pounding down on the foldout table he was using for a desk. He assaulted the table with such an inhuman amount of force that his punch actually left a crack all the way down the center, nearly splitting the entire table in two. His violent gesture had taken him by complete surprise, as had the degree of his rage toward Tom. Without the slightest bit of emotional repression left to hold him back, he was finally beginning to understand just how pure a death wish he'd developed for his brother.

Apparently he was so incensed that the violent impulse couldn't even leave his hand. The hand continued to shake long after he had intended. In fact, it was more than just a shake. `The shaking had suddenly become so violent that it was growing into something more like a tremor.`

Loki quickly latched onto his trembling right hand and tried to soothe it with his left. Maybe it was something muscular. A muscle cramp in the hand, perhaps from all his recent work at the computer. He worked at it strenuously, massaging the hand for two full minutes before the trembling finally began to subside. Or rather, not the "trembling," but the "cramp." That was surely all it was. Just a cramp.

Memo

From: L
To: QR2

We will deal with your mishandling of this
situation later. This step of OCS can wait.
Subject B is a much higher priority. Stand down
and await instructions. I will deal with Enigma.

"MOM?"

Heather jolted up slightly from her bed before a shot of excruciating pain forced her to fall flat on her back.

This Kind of Dark

"Mom?" she called again, keeping her neck as stiff as possible on the pillow to avoid the throbbing pain. "Mom, my back hurts. . . and my neck. . . . Mom?"

Her mother wouldn't answer. Why wouldn't she answer?

Because she's gone. Heather, wake up, you're asleep. No. You were asleep. Now you're awake. Fix your back. Your spine is cracking.

"No." Heather jolted in her bed and reached down for something to hold on to. The bed. She could hold on to the bed. She pressed her palms down on the bed and caressed the sheets. She could feel the sheets. That helped. It helped to feel the sheets. Maybe she was ready to feel around for the light switch.

A light switch won't help, Heather. Stop pretending you don't remember what's wrong with you. What time is it?

"I don't know," Heather uttered aloud. But she was awake enough now. She knew what she was doing. She was conversing with her own brain.

What do you mean, you don't know? Open your eyes and look at your watch.

"They *are* open. *Shhh.*" She needed to stop talking to herself.

The pieces were starting to fall back together now. All the crumbling little pieces. Her eyes were open now; she was sure of it. But she couldn't know whether the light was on or off. And she couldn't know what time it was because she couldn't see a clock. And she had no way of knowing if her mother was sitting right next to her asleep or if the room was completely empty.

"*Mom?*" She strained to make the loudest sound she could. "Mom, are you asleep?"

The silence was like no silence she'd ever heard. Because it was mixed with the black, black darkness. Not dark like nighttime. Not dark like a room with the lights off. In the nighttime, you still had some sense of where the sky was. In a dark room, you had some sense of the walls. But this was so different. This kind of dark just kept going. It just traveled out on all sides for miles and miles. It was like floating in outer space. . . but without the stars. Just pitch black space. No sound and no light. And barely any weight.

Mom already left. Don't you remember? They all left. The nurse said you were going to sleep, and the family went home. But how long ago was that? Two minutes? Two hours? It doesn't really matter, does it? Either way. . . you're alone in here.

She rubbed her hands over the sheets again. God, she wished there was something else to hold. Anything.

The family could have left her with something. A stuffed animal. A pillow that at least smelled like home. She should have made her mother stay. Why didn't she make her stay?

"Shhh," she scolded herself. "It's okay. You're okay. Shhh."

She'll be back. She'll be back in the morning, and she'll talk to you. And maybe Carrie will come in the morning. And Megan and Laura and Ed. And they'll talk to you. In the morning. How long can that be from now?

It could be hours, for all she knew. Or. . . maybe it *was* morning?

A sound! Finally a sound. What's that sound?

A sound had come from across the room. At last she could give the room a shape again. She'd forgotten where the walls were. But what was the sound? Two more seconds and she was sure. It was a door. A creaking door. A visitor! Maybe it really was morning? *Please, please let it be morning.*

"Mom?" she called out, feeling her voice strengthen. "Ed?"

"*Shhh,*" a voice insisted. Was it a man or a woman?

"Who is it?"

"It's okay," the voice whispered. It was a man's whisper. Whoever he was, he was coming closer. "You've got to stay quiet, okay?"

"Who is it?" Heather asked again. She could feel him standing at her bedside now.

"Heather, it's me," he said quietly.

Heather felt a wave of warm and gorgeous relief pass over her entire body. All her excruciating back and neck pain suddenly seemed to slip down to totally bearable levels. Her thoughts started to clear up again. The darkness became far less frightening. Because now he was close enough for Heather to hear him. Now, without the whispering, she could hear the deep and perfect tone of his voice. Now she noticed that his voice was just as stunningly handsome as his perfect jaw and his bluer-than-blue eyes. . . .

"*Josh?*" she squealed.

"Shhh," Josh warned her again. "We've got to stay quiet, Heather, okay? Can you do that for me? Because visiting hours just ended, and they'll kick me out if they hear."

"I'll stay quiet," Heather whispered with a joyful grin. "I promise."

"Good."

"Where have you been?" she groaned through a smile. "I've been waiting forever. Everything got so crazy at my house, I wasn't even sure what *happened* to you. God, I was so worried. And everything just got so blurry after a while, my thoughts, and. . . I just don't remember every—"

"*Heather,*" Josh interrupted, sounding frustrated. "I'm really serious about the quiet thing, *okay?*"

"Okay, I'm sorry," she whispered, placing her hand over her mouth with a smile. "I just. . . I'm so happy you're here. Everything hurts so bad, Josh. My back and my neck, and I can't think straight—I can't even tell when I'm talking or thinking. And I can't breathe so well—"

"I know," Josh said. "Don't worry. We're going to end all that right now."

"I just needed you here," she said, feeling overwhelmingly weepy all of a sudden. In all the darkness, her emotions had developed a mind of their own. "I'm sorry. I just. . . I needed another voice in the room."

"Well, I'm here," Josh said, "but Heather, I need you to be *superquiet* now, okay? We don't want the doctors coming in while I give you this."

"Give me what?"

"Just relax."

Heather suddenly felt Josh's hand grab onto her wrist and hold down her arm. And then she felt a sting on the inside of her elbow as he pulled something out of her vein. The IV.

"*Ow.* Josh, what are you doing?"

"It's okay," he said. "I'm going to give you something that'll end this miserable state you're in. Just stay quiet and don't move."

"Wait." Heather jolted slightly and grasped onto his hand, tugging to pull it off her wrist. She didn't like him holding down her arm. She didn't like how tight his grip was.

"*Heather,* just be cool, sweetie. Five seconds. I just need five seconds."

"No, wait," Heather whined. "Josh, I don't like it. Can we just—"

"Okay, just *shut up.*"

"I don't like it!" Heather howled quite suddenly. "I don't like it!" She couldn't even believe her own volume as her hands and arms began to jolt and spasm and flail to break free of Josh's grip.

"*Stop it,*" he demanded in a strained whisper.

"I'm scared, Josh. I'm *scared.*" She swiped her nails at his hands again and again as he battled to keep hold of her wrist. "What is it? What are you giving me? *What are you giving—*"

His strong hand clamped down over her mouth. It gripped the entire lower half of her face firmly, crushing her jaw with the pressure. She couldn't utter a sound.

"I said *shut up,*" he spat in a cold and vicious whisper. "Just keep your goddamn mouth shut so we can get this over with."

"TATIANA. . . CAN YOU HEAR ME?"

Now That She Was Dead

Tatiana had always wondered what angels would sound like. When she was six years old, she'd become obsessed with the angels at the Hermitage

Museum in St. Petersburg. She remembered staring up at all the red-cheeked cherubs sitting on their clouds painted on the ceiling and telling her mother that she looked just like them. *But what did they sound like?* she had wanted to know. She had thought that they might make music when they spoke or perhaps some kind of ethereal sounds, like whale songs or cooing birds. But finally, at the ripe old age of seventeen, she knew. Now that she was dead, she had just discovered that angels not only looked like her mother, they sounded like her, too.

"Tatiana?" her mother's voice called to her again. But this time it was tinged with the most disturbing high-pitched desperation and anxiety. Now the voice seemed to be funneled through a gigantic megaphone only inches from her face, reverberating so loudly through her throbbing skull that each consonant cut like a knife.

Knife. He stabbed you to death. Open your eyes and look. See if the knife is still stuck in your heart. Maybe your mother, the angel, will help you pull it out.

"Mama. . . ?" she whispered as her eyes slowly fluttered open.

"Oh, thank God," her mother cried in Russian. "I was starting to wonder if you were going to wake up."

Tatiana looked up and saw her mother's beautiful face hovering over her. "I—I don't. . . ," she stammered. "Is this heaven?"

"No, sweetheart," her mother said quietly, wiping

110

all the little hairs away from her forehead. "I'm afraid we are still here on the earthly plane."

"But..." Tatiana was deeply confused. "I'm not dead?"

Her mother's eyes widened with her smile as she shifted Tatiana's head from the pillow on the couch onto her lap. "You are so very far from dead," she explained. "We got here in time. God did us a rather large favor. You passed out. A nasty bump on the chin, that is all."

"And you're not dead?" She *did* look so much like an angel. How could she not be...?

"*No*, I am not dead. Not in the least."

"But what happened to him? Where's—"

"No more questions," her mother pleaded with deep concern in the tiny crinkles at the corners of her eyes. "Questions later, I promise. Now we rest and we wait to hear back from Tom. That is the best thing for now."

"Tom's not dead?"

"*Nobody* is dead," she explained with a slight laugh. "At least, not yet."

It might have taken a few extra questions, but Tatiana was finally grasping the realities piece by piece. She shot up from her mother's lap and wrapped her arms tightly around her neck, squeezing her again and again to feel every living muscle and bone in her body— every living hair on her head. She had no plans to let go anytime soon.

Her chin might feel like it had been split in two and her mouth might be almost too dry to speak, but all she could think about was everything Gaia had told her earlier that night.

You were right, Gaia. You were right. My mother is alive. And Loki is nothing but a sick and twisted liar.

"Now, sweetheart," her mother said, stroking her hair. "There is one question I need to ask you, okay?"

Tatiana nodded slowly in her mother's lap.

"Tatiana, Tom is out there right now searching for Gaia. We were very much hoping once you woke up that you might know where she is. Do you know? Do you have any idea where Tom will be able to find her?"

Tatiana tried to focus her brain well enough to remember her last meeting with Gaia. She remembered that Gaia was going to meet Ed for something, but the more she thought about it, the more she realized. She had been so preoccupied with all of her sulking for her mother, she had never even asked Gaia where she was going.

"I. . . don't know," she admitted. "I know she was going to meet Ed, but. . . I don't know *where.*"

She was suddenly stricken with a kind of guilt that hurt much more than her aching chin. Gaia had practically carried her all the way home on her shoulders earlier. Now Gaia was obviously still in grave danger, and Tatiana couldn't even begin to return the favor. She couldn't even point them in the right direction.

"Tom will find her," Tatiana said finally, trying to make herself believe it. "I'm sure he will find her." She believed it even less the second time.

No one would
be dying on
her watch.
No one.

not

god.

gaia.

"WHAT THE HELL IS TAKING YOU SO long?"

A deep, dull-witted voice had entered Heather's hospital room like some kind of gift from God. This was what she'd been praying for in the unbearable darkness. This was what she'd been begging

Fight or Flight

for again and again while Josh crushed her head against the pillow, gripping her arm as firmly as a cold steel shackle. She'd prayed for anyone. Anyone with *eyes*. Anyone who could stop him. Because she'd just about run out of fight, and she could only scrape desperately at his hands for just so much longer.

Josh quickly yanked his sweaty hand away from Heather's face.

She pulled in as much air as she could in the hopes of forcing a legitimate scream. Whoever had come into the room would surely hear her now. The voice she'd heard sounded hefty and deep. Whoever he was, he must be huge. He'd surely see her and tackle Josh—do something to pull him away from her. . . .

"Please." She wanted to scream out to the stranger, but there was so little air in her lungs, she could barely make a sound. "Please, he's trying to—"

Josh slapped his hand back down over her mouth. "Don't you make another sound," he whispered down to her. "I just need one more second," he said to the other man.

"Another second for *what?*" the dull voice replied.

"Just give me two seconds," Josh barked quietly.

"Oh, now it's two seconds?"

Heather's heart shrank down to nothing. The voice wasn't a doctor's or a custodian's or even an innocent passerby's. Somehow, in her total panic, she'd missed it at first. But now she understood. They were here together. And as Heather put together the sense of every word the stranger had said, she realized... he wasn't going to tackle Josh. He wasn't going to tug him away and beat him up, and he certainly wasn't going to call the police. Not only wasn't he going to stop Josh from murdering Heather, he thought Josh was taking *too long* to do it.

She was on her own. The only one fighting for Heather's life here would be Heather. There had to be a little more fight in her. There had to be one more shot of adrenaline she could squeeze out. That's what adrenaline was *for*. Fight or flight. And pinned down to a bed and too blind to even find the damn door, flight was definitely out of the question. So fight it would have to be.

She felt the sharp point of Josh's syringe touch the tender skin by her vein, and she gave it everything she had left. She followed her instincts and swatted hard, slapping her right hand at that very spot with all of her strength.

And she *connected*. She felt it. She'd made contact with something. It had to be the syringe, didn't it?

"*No*," Josh hissed, with frustration so intense, it bordered on desperation. She heard the faint sound of breaking glass on the floor from a few feet away. *Yes. You did it, Heather. You got it!*

"You *idiot*," Josh spat down at her in an almost inaudible whisper. "I was trying to *help* you."

Help her? What the hell was that supposed to mean?

"All right, come on," the deep-voiced stranger complained as Heather heard him moving closer. "We should have been out of here five minutes ago. Which one are you, anyway? One or Two? I don't know how he ever tells you freaks apart."

"I'm One," Josh muttered angrily.

One? What was Josh talking about? Nothing they said made any sense. Heather had thought she was thinking more clearly, but maybe she had it all wrong. Maybe her brain was cloudier than ever? What were they still doing here? She'd already swatted the thing away. *Please,* she begged to herself. *Please let this be over. Please let them leave.*

"Yeah, well, I'm going to tell him that Number One wasted a bunch of our time here," the man said. "How were you trying to do it? For Christ's sake, she's just *lying* there. I could have done this in two minutes. All you need is that pillow and it's totally untraceable. I don't know what *your* problem is...."

Heather felt her pillow getting yanked out from under her head. Her head fell back on the hard, flat mattress. *Scream, Heather. For God's sake, scream.*

But the next thing she knew, her entire face was completely smothered. It was like being forced underwater. Every orifice in her head had been shut off completely. She couldn't make the faintest sound. She couldn't take the smallest breath. She couldn't hear anything. All sound had been flushed down some black hole except for her heartbeat, which was pounding like some kind of techno nightmare.

She screamed silent, inaudible screams into the pillow again and again, trying to grab onto it, trying desperately to push it off her face, but it only made him push down harder. The entire front of her face had gone completely numb. Her nose felt like it might break, and her lips dug down against her teeth.

God didn't want to punish her with blindness. That must have been some kind of karmic mistake. God's plan was obviously for her to die. She'd somehow cheated her fate the first time around, just like Oedipus. That's what it had to be. She was supposed to die alone, suffering, and in pain. Ed had saved her from it the first time, but now it was for real. No more cheating. Death by asphyxiation. Without a single good-bye to friends or family. Untraceable. That would be her last thought. That her death was untraceable.

And then the pillow flew from her face. Literally. Like it had wings. Like God himself had changed his mind. Like he'd decided to issue a last minute reprieve and release every bit of pressure, sucking the pillow back into the sky. Heather heaved in air with a series of horribly painful coughs that shook her weak and unbearably sore chest to its core. Her eardrums nearly exploded from the sudden pressure change as sound came swelling back into her ears like a loud echo in reverse.

She suddenly felt a large tremor from the ground that momentarily shook the bed, and then finally she heard a voice. A voice that was only inches from her face.

"Heather, are you okay? Can you hear me? Can you breathe?"

"Who is that? Who's there?"

"It's Gaia," she said. Heather felt something plastic shoved into her hand and her thumb placed over a button. "Keep pressing that button, okay? Just keep pressing it. We need a nurse in here before I get my ass kicked."

It was all happening so quickly, Heather could hardly regain her orientation in the outside world. But she understood at least one thing.

Gaia had pulled the pillow from her face. Not God. Gaia.

HE MUST HAVE WEIGHED THREE HUNDRED

pounds. The entire floor shook when she flipped him to the ground. The first flip was easy because she'd taken

him by surprise. But his counterattack was going to be the hard part. His biceps were literally the size of Gaia's head.

Sure enough, the moment she'd gotten the nurse's pager to Heather, she felt his arms collapse around her chest, lifting her two feet off the ground and hurling her against the blank white wall like a bag of wet laundry.

"Ooompf." Her entire right side collided with the wall, crushing her arm into her rib cage and slamming her head against the wall like a hard rubber ball. She heard a piercing ring in her head as it bounced back off the wall and hit the floor.

"Gaia?" Heather called out. "Are you okay?"

Get up, Gaia. Get up now.

She launched herself up from her back onto her feet and landed in a defensive stance.

"I'm fine, Heather," she replied. "Just keep pressing that button."

There was no way he was getting in another easy shot like that one. Not as long as she could face him. Josh was of course right behind him. Whenever there was an attempted murder, Josh didn't seem to be too far behind. But why wasn't he coming at her?

Gaia couldn't think about that now. The enormous one was advancing again, and he was quick for someone his size. Quick and well trained.

He faked to her face and jabbed a hard blow to her gut, knocking her back against the wall. He snapped a high kick straight at her face, but she ducked right, swooping up and under and delivering a swift kick back to his nose. She drew blood, but he looked completely unfazed. Gaia realized that punches and kicks weren't going to do the trick.

She launched into a quick jump and roll and popped up by the two metal chairs in the corner. But he was right on her. He swung hard for her face. She sidestepped the punch and used his momentum to shove him the rest of the way straight into the wall. That one, unlike her punch, had hurt. She could tell from his pained grunt and from the massive dent his shoulder left in the wall. He flipped right around, though, and came back at her.

But now he was in the position she wanted him to be in. He was charging back at her, angry and disoriented. The two worst things to be in combat.

She stepped back to the chairs and waited for him to lunge, relaxing every muscle and freeing her brain of any and all distractions. *Focus now. . . .*

He came at her faster than she'd expected. But she was still ready for him. In one fluid motion Gaia crouched to the ground and kicked out, sweeping the man's legs out from under him as she grabbed onto the metal chair. As his entire three-hundred-pound frame fell face forward toward the floor, Gaia raised the chair high above her and brought it down mercilessly on his back and head with an unholy metallic crack. He was down for the count.

Good. Now she could focus on the real enemy.

She dropped the chair back on the ground and stepped toward Josh.

"Don't," he uttered. "You don't understand what's going on here."

"Oh, I understand exactly what's going on here, Josh, and I won't let it." She took another step toward him, and he took another step back. "No one else is going to die because of me," she explained. "*No one.* You tell him that's *it.* It's *done.*" She took one step closer and Josh lashed out. "Don't!" he shouted, jabbing his fist forward in a punch.

Gaia dodged the punch and latched both her hands onto his wrist, pulling his weight completely off balance and then flipping him hard to the ground, nearly twisting the entire arm out of its socket.

He let out a painful cry as his spine hit the linoleum, and Gaia couldn't help but take a certain vengeful pleasure in it. Josh deserved absolutely any punishment anyone could devise for him. He deserved so much worse than just to be flipped on his ass. In all honesty, Gaia truly believed he deserved to die. But she wasn't in this room to be his executioner. She was here to protect Heather from him. And that's what she had done.

Except. . .

As he lay there writhing in pain, Gaia's hands still

firmly clasped to his wrist, something unexpected caught her eye. She realized that her hands weren't the only things on his wrist.

There was a tattoo. A small black tattoo on his inner wrist.

QR1

Jesus. One of them. Gaia hadn't protected Heather from Josh. She'd protected Heather from one of Josh's *clones*. Now she was *really* pissed.

For one thing, she couldn't imagine what the real Josh was doing if Loki had sent a "qualified replicant" to kill Heather. But more than that, Gaia despised these genetic imitations of Josh almost more than she despised the man himself. Seeing that tattoo only made her flash back to those horrible nights when Josh and his "twin brothers" had all tag-teamed to mentally and physically torture her, taking her as close as she had ever come to the brink of insanity and nearly gutting Ed Fargo from head to toe. The more she thought about it, the harder she found herself gripping his wrist. And she couldn't help thinking. . . Given that he was really *wasn't* a human being, maybe it wouldn't be such a bad idea to put at least one of Loki's murderous living weapons out of commission. . . .

She never should have stopped to think. She felt a rock-hard kneecap hammer her spine, shooting her forward into the opposite wall as she tripped over QR1's body.

She spun around on the floor and saw the huge man towering above her. Apparently he wasn't down for the count. *Never take your eyes off them, Gaia. Remember that for the next time. If there is a next time. . . .*

He really was a huge bastard. And he was wielding one of the metal chairs high over his head. *No time to move.* This was going to hurt. This was going to hurt really bad. . . .

"Ms. Gannis?"

The three-hundred-pound thug let the chair fall to the ground with a deafening clatter as all heads turned to the doorway.

A young nurse had finally answered Heather's page. She stuck her head into the room with a look of complete shock. To Gaia's absolute disgust, for a split second the thug actually made a move toward the nurse. They really didn't care who they left in their wake, did they? But as the nurse let the door swing open the rest of the way, she revealed the mass of patients who had gathered in the hallway, all of them looking both terrified and fascinated as they tried to peer inside the room.

Too many witnesses. Gaia knew it. They weren't going to try anything else with all these witnesses. The patients must have all been gathering in that hallway, hearing the cries and thuds but too frightened to actually head inside. And with good reason.

"What's going on in here?" the nurse squeaked

with horror as Gaia and fake Josh picked themselves up off the floor. "Ms. Gannis, are you all right?"

"No," Heather cried, shaking her head as she stared up at the ceiling and tears fell from her eyes. "Nurse, please, I don't know these men. I don't know them and. . . and they're harassing me. Please get them out of here. *Please.*"

Heather was smarter than Gaia gave her credit for. She knew that if she'd started throwing words like *murder* around, they might not be so sure this little episode wasn't just another manifestation of her bizarre "symptoms."

The nurse turned her troubled eyes to the two men in the room. But before she could say anything, a rather large security guard stepped in behind her. He eyed the two men up and down, and suspicion, distrust, and anger began to register in his face.

"Gentlemen? Are we having a problem here?"

"Please," Heather cried. "I don't know how they got in here. Please get them out."

The guard stepped closer to them. "How *did* you get in here? You're not supposed to be in here."

"We do know her," fake Josh replied with his best attempt at a defusing smile. His thug accomplice made a pathetic attempt at a smile as well, but with a bloody nose and a huge lump on the back of his head, his credibility was way below zero. Besides, it was obvious the guard wasn't the least bit interested in hearing a story. He eyed both of them one more time, and that was clearly enough for him.

"You and you," he said, pointing a stern finger at each of them. "You're out of here. *Now.* I'm escorting you out of this hospital. And I don't want to see you *back* in this hospital, you understand?"

He placed his hand over the holster of his gun just to be clear. But they weren't going to bother putting up any resistance at this point. Loki would surely find some other way to infiltrate. But this particular attempt was officially history.

Gaia fixed a cold stare on each of them as they followed the guard out the door. She knew she would most likely see at least one of them again in the very near future. If and when she found Loki and confronted him, she had no doubt that QR1 and who knew how many other Josh clones would be close by. But for now, she was more than a little pleased to say her good-byes.

Once they were gone, she stepped back toward Heather to check on her, but the nurse was still standing in the room, looking generally concerned and perturbed.

"Miss?" She stared at Gaia and crossed her arms. "I'm afraid you'll have to go as well. Visiting hours are over and—"

"No, please," Heather pleaded from her bed. "Please. . . she's my sister. And she's been keeping me company, and. . . I'm kind of scared of being alone right now. Would it be all right if she stayed with me?"

Gaia turned back to the nurse and waited for her answer.

"Yes, of course," the nurse said. "Of course. I understand. She can stay."

"Thank you," Heather uttered, finally beginning to calm down a bit. "Thank you so much."

"All right, then." The nurse smiled. "You try to get some rest now, all right? Just rest. I'm sure your sister will take good care of you."

"Oh, I will," Gaia said. That was for damn sure. If the nurse hadn't allowed her to stay, they would have had to find Heather a new nurse. Because Gaia wouldn't be leaving Heather's side again. Not for two minutes. No one would be dying on her watch. No one.

The intensity in Gaia's eyes seemed to make the nurse a little uncomfortable. She smiled a slightly awkward smile and then said good night, closing the door behind her.

Finally Gaia and Heather were alone in the room. No thugs, no clones, no doctors, no nurses.

And finally Gaia could admit that she was about ten seconds from blacking out completely. She let down her strong face and slumped over. She stumbled to the other vacant bed in the room and collapsed on top of it, sprawled out in a diagonal, her shoes dangling over the side.

"Heather," she muttered out of the side of her mouth. "The thing about me is. . . sometimes after a

126

fight. . . I need to pass out for a little while. So I'm going to pass out for a little while now."

"Gaia, wait," Heather begged. "Do you think. . . Could you stay awake for just a little while longer? I was. . . kind of losing it in the darkness and the silence, and now, after everything I've been through tonight, I really don't think I can take much more of it. Not just yet. Could you stay up with me for a little while?"

Gaia checked her body. The room was definitely getting dimmer, and her eyelids were most definitely fluttering. But she could stay awake for a while longer. If she focused hard enough, she was sure she could do it for Heather. Gaia knew all about the darkness and the silence. They weren't her favorites, either.

"Okay," Gaia muttered from her totally flat-faced position on the bed. "I can make it—don't worry."

"*Thank you,*" Heather intoned, sounding genuinely thrilled that Gaia would stick it out with her. "I don't know what would have happened if you hadn't shown up, Gaia. No, I do know what would have happened. I'd be gone. God, I'm so lucky you were still here. What were you still doing here?"

Gaia felt a twinge in her chest at the question. She was so exhausted, she wasn't even sure whether the twinge was good or bad. Was it the physical memory of finally being back in Ed's arms, or was it another painful pang of guilt at having stolen a genuine moment of joy while Heather was living out a nightmare right down the hall? Whichever it was, Gaia had fewer and fewer regrets about her time in the closet with Ed. Not only could she not wait for the next time she'd see him again, but she was also beginning to feel far less guilty about it. After all, if they hadn't spent their time in the closet and if Gaia hadn't decided, after her few minutes of private thinking time, to check one last time on Heather. . .

"I was just. . . straightening some things out," she said, opting to keep things nice and vague for now.

"Well, thank you, Gaia," Heather said, sounding deeply grateful to the point of tears. "Thank you *so much.* I just wish I could see you right now. I wish I could look you in the eye and thank you for saving my life."

She *had,* hadn't she? Gaia had saved Heather's life. She had been so busy fighting, she hadn't really thought about it in those terms. And she couldn't help thinking that maybe this was some kind of karma? Giving in to Ed earlier. Saving Heather tonight. Maybe, in some strange cosmic way, Gaia had finally found a way to make up for nearly getting Heather killed that night in the park? Maybe everything was coming full circle tonight. Heather even seemed to be getting some of her lucidity back. Maybe it helped to know that she was no longer on her own.

"Seeing is overrated," Gaia said, trying to at least flop herself onto her back. "I mean, what's there really to see? I'll tell you what. I'll close the curtain around my bed, and then I won't be able to see you, either. We'll be even."

Heather seemed to consider this suggestion for a

second. "You really are a freak, aren't you," she concluded.

"Yes, and. . . ?" It went without saying that Gaia was a freak.

"And I am, too," Heather said.

"*Oh,* yeah," Gaia agreed. "Big freak."

"We'll be *even.*" Heather repeated it to herself quietly as if she were savoring it. "I like that. We *are,* Gaia," she said, with an odd tone of official declaration. It sounded like her mind might be falling a little out of sync again. "We're even. Okay? From now on? Even."

"Even," Gaia agreed, half asleep. "Just give me two seconds to get blind." Gaia hoisted herself up and tugged the dark blue plastic curtain all the way around her bed, dropping back down on the pillow as the notion of staying awake became more and more of a fantasy.

"Heather, I'm sorry, but I think I have to sleep a little, okay? I really think we're safe in here tonight. We've got the guard out there, and I don't think Loki is going to hit the same place twice in one night. So let's just try to relax. Heather. . ."

Gaia heard a faint snore coming from the other bed. Heather must be just as exhausted as she was. How could she not be after everything they had been through in this interminable day of horrors? They'd both basically been fighting off death almost hour by hour, and somehow or other. . . they'd both won. At least for today. They deserved at least one good night's sleep. They had earned it.

TOM FELT A TWINGE IN HIS SPINE

the moment he saw it. He'd barely pulled his car up to George's Perry Street town house when he felt the spark of pain ignited by the sight of a simple piece of yellow plastic.

Yellow Plastic

Police tape.

All he'd seen was the crime scene tape floating in the wind, broken in two pieces on either side of George's front door. And he already knew.

He knew what had become of George Niven. And he finally understood what that grinning little bastard on the fire escape had meant when he said, "Why don't you ask your buddy George?"

Because Tom knew his brother. He knew what Loki did to people who'd outlived their usefulness. And George should have known it, too.

Why did you do it, George? How could you be so foolish? We watched him operate for years. Didn't you know where it would lead? Didn't you know what he'd do to you? God, George, were you my last hope for finding Gaia tonight?

Those were just a few of the hundreds of questions Tom had for George. And questions were only the beginning of what Tom had planned, to be followed by the most scathing brand of verbal abuse and then, most likely, unless George had some kind of earth-shattering explanation, some form of severe physical punishment. Nothing deadly, much as Tom's most vengeful self might have wanted it, but certainly something to ensure that George felt the appropriate amount of regret for what he'd done. And then an immediate interrogation. Squeezing out every bit of knowledge George might have had about Gaia's whereabouts.

But Tom was already rather sure that none of his questions would ever be answered. And as for George's punishment, it appeared someone had already taken care of that.

Now Tom had been forced to shift gears completely. And his heart was no different than any other engine. If it wasn't prepared to shift gears, it was going to stall. All those years of trust and faith and admiration for his friend. And a few days of despising him. Tom didn't know what to feel. But no amount of speculation or confusion was going to stop him from going inside. He had to see it for himself. He needed some kind of visual confirmation other than one yellow piece of plastic.

He climbed the stone steps as he fished for his spare key to George's place, but when his hand grabbed the knob, he realized that the door was unlocked. Someone had done all of this already. Someone had broken the tape, unlocked the door, and ventured inside. And they hadn't bothered to lock it when they left.

Gaia. It had to be. She'd been here and gone *already.* When? Tonight? Days ago? Maybe there was some clue inside?

Tom walked into the dark apartment, feeling that eerie

sense of stillness—his least favorite part of the job. Even to this day, he despised the sensation of walking through a crime scene. That sense that nothing in the room pertained to the present anymore. Everything in this house was now a part of the past. The George and Ella Niven Museum. A study in betrayal and poor judgment.

Tom climbed the stairs to the top floor and flipped on the hallway light. He immediately began checking the rooms, doing a quick cursory glance in each bedroom. But it didn't take very long. He found what he was looking for on his third opened door. Gaia's bedroom. The flash of stark white lines contrasting with the dark floor had caught his eye instantly. He flipped on the light in the room and confirmed his first fear from the moment his car had pulled up to the house. An outline of a body in white tape. Bloodstains that had turned from red to black.

And only now did he realize the real reason he'd needed to see it. Because before he'd even had a chance to truly take in the image, he'd already found himself kneeling next to what was left of George Niven, his greatest friend of more than twenty years. White tape and black smudges of dried blood. That was all that remained of George. And although Tom's heart might have been too hardened for him to cry at this point, he suddenly realized why he had made himself enter this house.

It wasn't just to settle his confusion. It wasn't just to confirm what he'd already known the moment he

132

arrived or even to find another clue about Gaia. He knew there were no more clues. It was none of those things.

Tom had come into this house to mourn.

The human heart was indeed a most bizarre phenomenon. He'd come here with nothing but spite and scorn in his heart. He'd come here to punish George, to hurt him if he had to, to force the truth out of him about Gaia and where Tom could find her. But the moment he had realized that George was dead. . . he'd come in to forgive him.

I'll never understand it, he thought as he knelt by the closest thing there was right now to George's grave. *I'll never understand why you did it. But in all honesty, in spite of all my rage and all my vengeful impulses, do you know what I really believe in my heart of hearts, George? I should be locked up in an insane asylum for this. . . but I honestly believe that you somehow thought you were doing good. However horribly misguided your judgment, however stupid and shortsighted and naive and idiotic you were, I believe you thought you were somehow being. . . noble. I suppose that makes me almost as much a fool as you. But that's how I'm going to choose to remember you. I'm going to remember you for all the noble things you did in your life—and there were many. And the rest of it. . . I don't think I'll ever forget what you did to us—what you did to my family. But I'll forgive you, George. I do forgive you.*

I just wish I could understand how it happened. I wish I could have been standing in the room the moment you decided to sell me out. We were like brothers, George. How could you turn on me like that when we were practically. . . ?

The thought was almost laughable. It was even too absurd a thought for Tom to finish. How could a brother turn on his own brother? Was he seriously asking himself this question? He'd thought he stopped asking that idiotic question ten years ago. Because it was about ten years ago that he'd realized the answer.

He'd discovered it while reading a book that he'd found in his motel room one night in Dallas, Texas. A little book called the Bible. While skimming through that very familiar book, it had finally occurred to Tom that a brother's betrayal wasn't such a mystery after all. In fact, judging from this *very* old book, he thought it was one of the oldest traditions in human nature. Cain and Abel. Jacob and Esau. Joseph and his brothers. . .

The conclusion was simple enough, and if George was any indication, it still held true today.

A brother's betrayal wasn't so uncommon at all. It was a brother's *loyalty* that seemed to be the real rarity. What a very, very sad thought.

Tom rose and stepped back from the ghostly outline. He had nothing left to say. And Gaia was still his only priority. He'd spoken his piece, and now it was time to move on.

He made his way down the stairs and out the front door in seconds. But the moment he sat down in his car, he realized. . .

George had been his only hope. He had no leads, not one message on his Blackberry. The Agency still didn't have a thing. Not a thing.

Tom blew out a long, frustrated sigh. He was getting so very tired. There was nothing in the world more exhausting than failure. It seemed he had already reached that dreaded moment that always seemed to present itself with his tragically independent daughter. That moment when he was utterly impotent. When he was drowning in his own futility. That moment when he realized yet again that Gaia's life was entirely in her own hands.

Ten o'clock tomorrow. . . Did it mean anything? Did Gaia have any idea about ten o'clock tomorrow? Did she have any idea what might happen to her tonight?

Tom had no more choices. If he was to be of any use tomorrow morning, he'd need to get some sleep tonight. He'd need to believe that Gaia had found herself a safe place to stay. In essence, he'd need to ignore that little voice in his head telling him that place didn't exist.

How could
Gaia possibly
have known
that
Heather
Gannis
was in
fact
remarkable?

the

tao

of

gwyneth

WAS SHE REALLY DREAMING OF

Grease and Potatoes

creaking doors and slow, haunting footsteps? She could have sworn they'd both been invading her subconscious for hours. How bizarre and preposterous would that be? Where were the images coming from, those cliché slice-and-dice summer blockbusters? What was next? The monster under the bed? The headless ghost of St. Vincent himself roaming the hospital in the wee hours of the morn? The lone severed hand crawling through the hospital, looking for hippies and sexually active teens?

For someone with no fear, there was nothing on this planet more ineffectual than a bad dream ripped off from a lame horror movie.

But there was another footstep. . . .

You're not dreaming, Gaia. You're awake. There's someone in this room.

This would of course be the part in the movie where she was supposed to stare into the camera, widen her eyes to comical proportions, and then scream bloody murder at least two or three times. But Gaia was nothing other than thrilled.

Whoever that someone was, he had been idiotic enough to think that opening a creaky door slowly was a stealthy way to enter a room. But all he had done was give her more time to plan the specific nature and duration of his beating. She'd *known* staying with Heather was the right choice.

She raised her chest gently to a more upright position and stared with anticipation at the blue plastic curtain she had closed around her hospital bed. She couldn't *believe* this was his best attempt at a sneak attack. It was pathetic. The faint light from the hallway was projecting his entire silhouette right through the curtain as he took each cartoonish step.

I hope it's you, Josh. I hope they didn't send that cheap imitation this time. Because you're the one I want. I have so been looking forward to this. . . .

Gaia flexed her fists and switched to a deeper focus. She would start with one perfectly placed shot to that repulsive face. And then she would improvise from there. Just one step closer. . . *Open the curtain. . . . Come on, asshole, open the curtain. . . .*

He finally slipped his fingers through the opening in the curtain. And the second he swung that thing open, she cracked his face with a lightning quick jab that knocked him flat on his coldhearted ass.

"You call that a sneak attack?" she taunted, shooting up from the bed onto her feet. "That is *pathetic,* you spineless little turd. *Pathetic.*"

"*Shhh. Jesus* freaking *Christ,*" he moaned from the floor, writhing around with his hand clamped over his eye. "Don't be afraid to tell me how you *really* feel. . . ."

Gaia looked down at him again. Only this time, she looked a little closer. Actually. . . it was the first time she had really looked at all.

"Ed. . . ?"

"No," Ed groaned quietly from the floor. "I go by 'Spineless Turd' now. *Christ*, you can punch. . . . *Owww*."

"Oh my God, *Ed*." Gaia collapsed down to the floor and cradled Ed, helping him up to a seated position. "I am *so sorry*. I thought you were. . . Wait a minute. How the hell did you know I was here?"

"I *know* you," he said with a sigh. "I knew you would stay over the second you said you were going to check in on Heather again. I would only have been surprised if you *weren't* here. Face it, Gaia. You're a compulsive savior."

"Gaia. . . ?" Heather interjected with a deeply groggy voice. Waking from hospital sedation had been known to take hours. Gaia didn't even know what kind of dose they were giving the poor girl, but it must have been just a step above horse tranquilizers. "Gaia, are you okay? What's happening?"

Gaia quickly propped Ed against the bed and leapt up to Heather's side.

Heather was still so utterly freaked out by her earlier attack, Gaia could hear the anxiety in her voice, even under heavy sedation. And why wouldn't she still be freaked out? Gaia was probably the only person in the world who wouldn't be.

She couldn't stand to see Heather like this. She honestly would have done just about anything to be back in school again, looking at Heather standing right in front of her, her hair hanging with that disgustingly perfect lilt as she bombarded Gaia with scathing insults about her poor hygiene and her choice of pants. Or perhaps she'd be engaged in one of those unbearable high-pitched group giggles with the FOHs. Anything would do. Any offensive scenario. Just as long as Heather could *see* it.

"It's okay, Heather," she assured her. "It's okay. It's just Ed."

"Ed?" Heather whimpered with a faint smile. "Ed's here? What time is it?"

Gaia turned back to Ed with a sudden disapproving glare. Hadn't they *specifically* agreed to refrain from any further contact until tomorrow? Had Ed just *forgotten?* "Yeah, Ed, what the hell time is it?"

"Oh my God," he moaned, gently removing his hand from his eye. "First of all, can we please keep it quiet so I don't get thrown out of here? Second, where is the love, Gaia? Can I get a *wee* bit more sympathy for your judo death chop before you go *Gaia* on me?"

He had her on the judo death chop thing. She knelt back down in front of Ed and examined his wound. She touched her finger gently to the little red welt above his eye.

"It's a little after midnight," he whispered, pretty

much disarming every one of Gaia's verbal weapons and defense mechanisms with his one and a half dark brown eyes and his scruffy head. "I brought snacks," he added.

He pointed his finger at a spot next to the door, where there was a small plastic shopping bag with the handles tied together. "Veselka," he said. "I got potato pancakes, vegetable soup—"

"Ed, what are you talking about?" Gaia squeaked quietly. "We can't have a sn—"

"*Rice Krispies Treats. . . ,*" Ed interrupted, staring reverently at the bag.

Gaia froze and looked back at the bag. "You sneaky bastard," she whispered, beginning to salivate at the thought of a hunk of butter, sugar, and dried rice. Not to mention the potato pancakes. . . There was no greater use of grease and potatoes than the potato pancakes at Veselka. Ed was no fool. He knew what he was doing.

Gaia wished she could find the strength to send Ed home. She didn't want him in this dangerous room. She didn't want to rub their incredibly recent reconciliation in Heather's face. She didn't want her and Ed getting caught and thrown out of the room, leaving Heather in here all alone again and vulnerable. . . .

"You guys. . . ?" Heather croaked. "Can I have a snack?"

Something about Heather's request for a snack nearly broke Gaia's heart.

But it was Ed's confident smile that sealed the deal. He knew Gaia could no longer say no. He knew that Gaia wouldn't dare deprive Heather—who was deprived right now of just about everything else in this world—the pleasure of a snack. She wasn't that cruel.

What he might not have known was that his bringing a midnight snack was probably the kindest, sweetest, most remarkable thing anyone had ever done for her since the age of twelve.

"Okay," she whispered, doing everything in her power not to grin with gleeful relief that Ed Fargo was back in her life. "One snack. But if they find us in here, then—"

"Oh, no, not in *here*," Ed corrected her.

Gaia stared into his mischievous, if mildly swollen, eyes. "What do you mean, not here?" she asked flatly.

"Can I have my snack now?" Heather chimed in.

"Hold on, Heather," Gaia replied impatiently before turning back to Ed. "Tell me now or you lose the other eye—"

"Okay, okay," he said, grabbing her wrist and lowering her hand.

God. Could she possibly be more embarrassed about how much she enjoyed just having his hand around her wrist? Gaia still couldn't quite fathom what had slowly begun to happen to her regarding one Edward Fargo. Deprived of him for so unbearably long, it seemed that upon his return, she had begun to develop a thoroughly over-the-top, ultracheesy, schoolgirl-crush-style infatuation for her best friend. Wasn't the infatuation supposed to come first? Before the sex? Before the friendship, even?

It was just another example of Gaia's life being in reverse as usual, but in this case it wasn't necessarily such a bad thing.

"I used to have to come to this hospital all the time to be tortured," Ed explained. "So I figured out some of the better places to be alone—as in, to hide. And there was only one place where they never found me."

"Uh-huh. . . ?"

Ed stretched his head over Gaia's shoulder, keeping his hand wrapped around her wrist. "Hey, Heather, do you feel like some fresh air?"

Gaia slapped her hand quietly against Ed's chest, chiding him with her eyes. "What are you talking about?" she whispered. "Heather can't just walk outside. She's hooked up to an IV. I don't even know if she can *walk*."

"IVs roll," Ed argued. "And so do people." He pointed again, this time to the other side of the door, where Gaia hadn't noticed a folded-up wheelchair. "A fine model," he said. "One of my personal favorites. Great traction. Cruise control. Zero to sixty in roughly fifteen to twenty minutes. Top of the line." Ed stepped over to the closet and pulled Heather's coat off the hanger. "So what do you say, Heather? A brief journey?"

"Have you guys ever had hospital food?" Heather asked.

"Uh. . . yeah?" Ed replied.

"*Right,*" Heather said, her hands shaking slightly as she raised her voice. "Then you can understand why all I really care about right now. . . is my snack."

"Very good." Ed smiled. "Well, then let's get you up," he said, turning to Gaia. "We're going to the roof."

"DO YOU HAVE EVERYTHING PREPARED for tomorrow morning?"

Loki was standing at the window of the shoddy Brooklyn apartment. He stared out at the street full of boarded-up brownstones, lit only by the one streetlamp that hadn't been shattered by some bored lowlife with a rock in his hand. He could barely remember why he'd ever cared for New York. Was it because he'd been born here? Probably. But that was in his prephobosan life, a life he hardly cared to remember.

A Rattle- snake's Tail

He turned back to Dr. Glenn, who was staring at him from behind the cracked desk. "*Dr. Glenn?* Are you listening to me? I asked you if we were prepared for tomorrow!" Still no reply. Loki's frustration doubled.

"Doctor! What is the matter with you? Have you gone *deaf?*" Loki smashed his hand next to the window, punching a gaping hole into the cheap drywall as bits and pieces crumbled to the floor. He quickly grabbed his shaking hand and soothed the cramp out of it until the extremely annoying tremors stopped.

"I am not deaf," the doctor said, focusing his worried, analytical stare at Loki's hand. "But I am extremely concerned, and I need you to start listening to me. You have been ignoring my warnings for the past three hours, and I hope you have noticed that the symptoms have only gotten progressively worse in that time."

"Nonsense," Loki spat back. "You don't know what you're talking about. A few minor cramps in my hands. My body is just adjusting to the drug."

"Do you want me to get a mirror?" the doctor asked. "Your face is crawling with facial tics. Can't you feel the right side of your mouth twitching?"

"Don't be ridiculous."

"Haven't you noticed your complete lack of emotional control?"

"I've freed myself of fear-induced repression."

"They're all side effects," the doctor insisted. "*Extremely severe* side effects."

"Stop exaggerating, Doctor, you're frustrating me."

"Why would I exaggerate? What reason would I have to lie to you?"

"*Jealousy,* for one," Loki barked, pounding his hand

against the wall again and then latching onto it with his other hand to smooth out the tremors. "It's a natural psychological phenomenon, Doctor. I see it all the time. We insult the things we envy. We nitpick and we criticize whatever it is we cannot be ourselves."

The doctor stepped much closer and took Loki's wrist in his hand. "Your pulse is racing," he said.

"I'm *excited*." Loki chuckled dismissively. "We've run into snags tonight, but things are finally moving smoothly. This will all be done with by tomorrow."

Loki pulled his wrist back, but the doctor wouldn't let go. "Doctor... let go of my wrist."

"Not until you take a good look at it."

"Let go of me, Doctor..."

"Look at your wrist."

Loki's eyes darted down to his wrist, which was trembling in the doctor's hand `like a rattlesnake's tail`. "I said let *go*." Loki shoved the doctor back two feet into the opposite wall.

The doctor regained his balance and took a few steps away from Loki. "Listen to me now," he said gravely. "Phobosan II is not even close to being ready for trial usage. In fact, judging by the inordinate speed at which the side effects are progressing, it's clear to me that the second generation of the drug is far more dangerous than the first. I strongly recommend, in fact, I *insist* that you be administered the counteragent to the drug immediately."

Loki stepped toward the doctor with an incredible degree of menace in his eyes. "*You* do not insist, Doctor, is that clear? The only person in this room permitted to insist upon anything is *me*. And I will tell you what this mild little symptom is. It is a slight muscle spasm, that's what it is. So you will provide me with a simple prescription for muscle relaxants, and we will be done with it. I *insist*."

The doctor took another step back and reached into the pocket of his lab coat, producing a small vial in the palm of his hand. "Please," he said calmly. "I won't insist, then. I will only plead with you, as a scientist and as the doctor who is responsible for the current state you're in and every state that will follow. I only ask that you listen to what I have to say."

Loki sighed impatiently and thrust his troublesome hand into his pocket to keep it still. "You've got thirty seconds."

"Sir, please listen," Dr. Glenn said, trying to speak as quickly as possible to stay within his allotted time. "This one vial in my palm is the last remaining vial of the counteragent that we currently have, which is *extremely* odd considering the fact that I had *two* vials only hours ago. I may have misplaced one; I don't know. But this being the last vial of the antidote only makes the situation that much more urgent. You need to understand—it takes a considerable amount of time to produce this counteragent, and I have yet to teach the exact formula to the other doctors on the team. That means this one vial is extremely, extremely valuable, and sir, given that vials seem to be disappearing, I am telling you that you *want* to take this counteragent right now before there are any incidents or accidents and there is suddenly no counteragent to take. Muscle relaxants will do absolutely *nothing* for you. And I can already predict for you what the next stage after this one will be. These spasms and tics are going to continue to progress at a rapid speed until paralysis begins to set in and then quite possibly coma, if not death. And sir, while the worst symptoms *might* not kick in for as much as a month, judging from the current rate of mental and physical deterioration, I am honestly afraid that these symptoms could set in as soon as the next twelve hours, if not sooner."

"Yes," Loki said with a smile. "Well, that is just precisely the point, Doctor. *You* are afraid. And *I* am not."

"No, I don't think you—"

"I heard every word!" Loki snapped. "And now *you* will listen to *me*, Doctor. Here is what you are going to do. First, you will put that pitiful little vial back in your pocket or you can destroy it, I don't care. Then you will answer my initial question. And once you have answered that question, you will run along to your lab and you will fetch me a bottle of muscle relaxants. Is that all clear enough for you?"

"Sir—"

"*First*. . . you will put that vial *back* in your pocket."

Loki took a large step toward him, and Glenn finally dropped the vial back in his lab coat pocket.

"Good. *Now*, you will answer my initial question. *Is* everything ready for tomorrow morning?"

"Sir, I just think—"

Loki's hand shot out of his pocket and lunged forward, grasping the doctor firmly around the neck as he slammed him up against the wall. "*Enough!*" he growled, pulling tighter on his neck. "You don't speak out of turn anymore. You don't talk back again. You *shut* your sniveling cowardly mouth unless you are asked a question. And *when* you are asked a question, Doctor, you *answer* it, or else I will continue to squeeze your flimsy little windpipe harder. . . and harder. . . ."

Loki watched as the doctor's head shook more and more violently in his grip. He couldn't even tell if it was the doctor's pathetic fear making him shake or his own wildly convulsive hand holding his neck. Probably both.

"All right," the doctor choked out.

"All right?" Loki double-checked. "You're ready to answer my question now?"

"Ready," he said, his face turning a bright shade of red.

"Good." Loki let go of the doctor's neck and watched as he nearly collapsed to the floor. "So then. . . is everything ready for tomorrow morning?"

"Yes," the doctor answered simply, keeping ten full

paces between them and massaging his neck. "Yes, we're ready to go."

Finally, the simple answer Loki had been waiting for. "Well, I'm glad to hear it. Fine work, Doctor. Now, get along to your lab and get me some muscle relaxants. Something nice and strong."

"Yes, sir," the doctor muttered submissively as he backed his way toward the door.

"Perfect. And when you're done with that, you get yourself a good night's sleep. We've got a big day tomorrow."

Loki opened the door for the doctor and then slammed it behind him. He put his right hand back into his pocket, but then the left hand began to shake slightly. Not a problem. He was quite sure the doctor would hurry with those pills.

WHAT AN IDEAL TIME FOR A PICNIC.

Heather was at death's door. Loki was enjoying a free-range reign of terror. Ed and Gaia had sworn to stay away from each other for the night. And nurses and security guards would most likely be storming the roof shortly

Romantic Movies

to arrest the two of them for kidnapping an innocent blind girl from her hospital bed. So there was really only one legitimate way to cope with that much catastrophe and doom.

Rooftop snacking. Greasy after-hours East Village fare, Cokes from the hospital soda machine, a bizarrely cold night, and a bizarrely large moon.

Gaia had sat herself down on the ledge of the desolate, tarred-over roof and clutched her potato pancake in both hands, eating it like a bunless hamburger as she stared out at the lit-up cityscape and the damn near cartoon moon. Fried grease and salty potato fluff had never tasted so delicious. Most likely because it was a gift from Ed.

Yes, Ed had "provided" for her. And Gaia was too tired to pretend that didn't feel like a very small gift from God. She hadn't known until biting into the pancake just how starved she had been, not only for food, but for just a morsel of semitraditional human caretaking. *Not* that she *needed* anyone to take care of her. But how many times was she supposed to prove that fact before its rather obvious falsehood began to seep through the cracks of reality? Tonight she was in the mood to admit—to herself, that is—that ten minutes of being cared for could induce more absurd euphoria than ten *days* of self-sufficiency. No matter how much her life seemed to suggest the contrary, Gaia was in fact a human seventeen-year-old girl-person living on the planet Earth, who needed just exactly what the rest of the human girl-people needed. And that included the occasional thoroughly unexpected offering of greasy potato fluff by someone with eyes as kind and brown as Ed Fargo's.

Moonlight on a black-tarred hospital roof, Ed scrunched up next to her on the ledge with a can of Coke, and Heather quietly munching her own potato pancake as she sat in her wheelchair and ignored the rolling IV cart hanging over her head—assuming Loki's attempts at mass extermination were far from over, this might just be as romantic as Gaia's life was ever going to get. And that didn't bother her one bit.

She found about as much identification with the clichés from romantic movies as she did with the ones from the scary movies. She wasn't exactly planning to roll down any grassy hills with Ed anytime soon, or sit out on the porch swing, or tussle in the waves of some stretch of white beach, or go ice skating hand in hand at Rockefeller Center. . . .

Actually. . .

She wouldn't really have minded doing any of those things. In fact, she had to admit—to herself, that is—that she would, quite secretly, die to do any of those things with Ed. But as long as she could feel his thick shoulder leaning up against hers on the ledge. . . well, then moonlit black tar and predeath grease was more than enough romance.

"Mmph," Gaia grunted, speaking cavewomanese as she held up the pancake to indicate her enjoyment to Ed. Ed tilted his head slightly and took a bite.

"Mmph," he agreed as the two of them focused intently on the moon as if its blurred gray face was in the middle of telling some immensely entertaining story. "Now you're glad I came, right?"

Gaia kept her eyes fixed on the moon.

"Okay, I know I wasn't supposed to come," he admitted, "but. . . well, I mean, you were obviously hungry, or you wouldn't be eating that thing like some Parisian wolf-child. . . ."

"Napkin," Gaia said, holding out her hand. Ed leaned down, pulled a napkin out of the shopping bag, and handed it to her.

She swallowed down the last of her pancake and wiped her mouth thoroughly. And then she leaned forward and kissed Ed on the cheek, hoping that would explain her sentiments regarding the breaking of his promise.

Still no words, though. She was absolutely convinced that speaking any of the sentences in her head would produce enough cheese to make a large pizza.

Ed smiled with the satisfaction of having made the right choice with his late night visit. And then he kept his eyes fixed to hers. Gaia felt another twinge of guilt looking at the little purple knot that had formed over his eye.

"I can't believe I punched you in the face," she said.

"I deserved it," he said. "What kind of idiot sneaks up on Gaia Moore?"

Good point.

"I've still got a few things to learn in this relationship," he added.

He thought *he* had a lot to learn? Gaia was about as ready for this relationship as she was for. . .

Nope. There was *nothing* she felt less confident about than being in this real, full-blown, actual relationship with Ed that had officially restarted three hours ago. It was par for the course in The Life of Gaia: the thing she was the least prepared for had to be the thing she wanted the most.

"I. . . ," she began. *Cheese. Anything you're going to say. Just melted, processed, Velveeta cheese.* Now wasn't even the time for words, she reminded herself with tremendous relief. Not with Heather sitting right there in her own foggy little pancake world. "Heather, are you doing all right?" she asked.

Heather finished chewing and then stretched out her hand. The tremors in her hand were a vivid reminder of all that was waiting for them back in the real world below this roof. Gaia blinked hard and tried to stave off reality for just a few more minutes.

"Napkin?" Heather asked.

Ed grabbed another napkin from the bag and quickly stepped to Heather, kneeling before her and wiping her hand.

"I'm not *four*, Ed," Heather uttered with a weak half smile. "I'm just blind." She took the napkin from Ed and wiped her own hand.

"Right," Ed replied, shaking his head with complete embarrassment.

Gaia grinned. The truth was, for all the times she had seen Heather holding forth like a queen—followed by her bevy of doting attendants and drooling football monkeys, making royal pronouncements and spouting tidbits of wisdom from the tao of Gwyneth—Gaia had never been more impressed with Heather than she was at this moment. Hunched over in a wheelchair with a rolling IV drip, wiping potato grease from her trembling hand, and *still* dropping a little attitude bomb on Ed.

"I'm okay," Heather said, answering Gaia's question. "I like the air. And I like the food. And I *love* the company, believe me. Although Gaia. . . if that study in the sounds of silence is the best you can do with Ed, then you and I are going to have to sit down when all this is over and have a nice long talk about relationships."

Gaia nearly fell off the building. Partly from a degree of red-hot embarrassment she had never experienced in her entire life and partly from sheer amazement at Heather's nonvisual perception. Once again she had failed to give Heather Gannis enough credit. She hadn't just been sitting there in a blind and withering fog the entire time. Ever since Ed had walked into that room, some or all of her had been picking up everything Gaia and Ed were saying. . . and *weren't* saying.

But Heather deserved so much more credit than that. Gaia could honestly say that Heather was setting a stunning example.

When Gaia had watched Tatiana wallow in the darkest brand of self-pity earlier, she had assumed there was no other possible response to Loki's satanic maneuvers. It was certainly the best Gaia had been able to come up with time and again. But here was Heather, outdoing them both. Here she was, just marching through her blind fate with a half smile and resilience to spare. Loki was no longer even an issue for her. She had simply accepted her fate. Not cursed it or hidden from it or denied it. She had accepted that she couldn't see. So much so that she could joke about it to Ed. She'd accepted the end to their seemingly endless battles for Ed's affection, platonic or otherwise. So much so that she was giving *Gaia* relationship pointers. Remarkable. How could Gaia have possibly known that Heather Gannis was in fact remarkable?

All she knew now was that she would do everything in her power to protect her. And if there *was* a counteragent. . . if there was a cure out there for Heather. . . Gaia was going to find it.

"I'm really okay," Heather said, turning her vacant eyes toward Gaia and then back to Ed. "It's a beautiful night, isn't it? I can tell it is. I bet you can see the whole Village. You can, right? The whole thing?"

Ed stood up and looked over the ledge. "The whole thing," he said.

Gaia could hear him savoring the city almost as much as she did. She followed his eyes and looked out over Seventh Avenue, and Greenwich Avenue, and Twelfth Street, all of it looking like a strange, tasteful carnival bathed in amber streetlights.

"Tell me what you see," Heather said quietly.

"Greenwich is *packed*." Ed smiled, scanning his eyes down the street. "They really don't ever sleep, do they? You never think about it when you're down there. All the outdoor tables at Dew Drop Inn are full. Five homeys on the steps of the church. Gap, Starbucks, Starbucks, Gap. The clock on Jefferson Market Library. . . You can see the tops of the trees in Washington Square Park—"

"Okay, that's enough," Heather interrupted. "That's enough."

Gaia looked back at Heather and caught a glimpse of the pain she was working so hard to keep at bay. Hearing about the things she might never see again— the things they had all three taken for granted for so long—was too much for even the remarkable Heather. And it made Gaia's heart sink.

Gaia and Ed dropped their heads and stood still in silence. If Heather couldn't see it, they didn't want to, either. Gaia did her best to literally shake it off. Maybe it was time to go back downstairs and get a little more sleep.

Ed saw Gaia shake and took a step closer to her. "Are you cold?" he asked.

"No," she said. "I just—"

"*Yes*," Heather interrupted, replacing her sullen expression with one of frustration. "Yes, she is *a little* cold. Gaia, when the boy asks you if you're cold, you say *yes*. You say, 'Yes. I'm *a little* cold.' This leads to either old-fashioned chivalrous handing over of the jacket, or an arm around the shoulders, *or* the placing of the jacket over the shoulders and *then* the arm around the shoulders. God, what am I going to *do* with you? What *planet* are you from?"

Gaia and Ed stood there awkwardly, floating somewhere between mortified and delighted. And finally, out of deference to Heather, Gaia changed her mind.

"Yes," she said, "I am *a little* cold."

Ed dropped his head with embarrassment and then raised it with a smile of resignation. He removed his jacket as deliberately as possible, placed it over Gaia's shoulders, and then put his arm around her shoulders.

Gaia could feel her face turn bright red. Not because they had enacted this stupid transaction for a girl who couldn't even see, but because despite how ludicrously mechanical it had been, some very sick and diseased part of her had actually enjoyed the entire exchange. All they needed now was a porch swing to sit on. And of course, a large bucket in which to puke.

"Is his arm around you yet, Ga—"

"*Yes*," Gaia interrupted through clenched teeth.

"Well, okay, then," Heather announced. "Much better. Now I need to go downstairs. I'm really tired. . . ."

Gaia knew it was time to go back down. As much as she was enjoying Ed's visit, she and Heather still hadn't gotten half the sleep they needed to recover from the world's most harrowing day. It was time to go to bed.

Ed took hold of Heather's chair and led them back downstairs.

Gaia and Ed got Heather back into bed and said their simple good nights—the night had been complicated enough as it was. Finally Gaia laid her head back on the Clorox-scented hospital pillow. And she found herself saying her first bedtime prayer in ten years. It was an atheistic prayer, directed toward whoever or whatever answered the prayers of nonbelievers. She prayed that the morning would be just like this night. Because she knew the patterns of her life all too well. And the mornings were always so much worse than the nights. Always.

Memo

From: Anonymous relay 377FJC
To: Enigma

Must be brief. Risking my life to provide the
following information. 10:00 A.M. Thirty minutes from
now. Your daughter will be at St. Vincent's Hospital
on Seventh Avenue, visiting a patient named Heather
Gannis. She will be on the third floor. Room 305. Be
there by ten. If you are not there by ten, I can
promise you nothing. Except this: You will most
likely never see your daughter again.

White walls,
white
lights,

another

white

dead

sheets,
and

promise

white

coats. . .

WHO IS DR. GLENN?

For some strange reason, that question was the first on Gaia's mind as she began to wake. "*Began* to wake" was definitely the appropriate phrase, as she was so utterly groggy, she knew it would be

Raving Psychopath

one of those mornings when it took her an hour of pressing the snooze button before she could even lift her head from the pillow.

The offensive talk radio was already driving her insane. She wanted to reach over to her alarm to turn it off, but she couldn't even get her numb arm off the side of the bed to pound the button. She must have slept on it again. She *hated* when that happened. And could her room be any brighter? She must have forgotten to close the shade again. Or maybe Tatiana forgot to close it. Hadn't Gaia told her a million times that she despised the morning sun?

"Dr. Glenn, can I just double-check this with you?"

Dr. Glenn again. Who the hell was Dr. Glenn? Was he some annoying new talk show host?

"Tatiana," Gaia croaked through her dry and crusty mouth. "Can you *please* turn that off? I can't move my arm. And will you *close* the damn shade, please? How many times do I have to tell you?"

"Who is she talking to?"

"Oh, don't worry—that's to be expected. That's just the sedatives wearing off."

"What?" Gaia muttered, trying to fight off the bright light and adjust her eyes. "Are you talking to me? Tatiana? Natasha?"

"Don't worry, Ms. Moore," a woman's voice said rather loudly. "You're doing just fine. We'll have you out of here in a jiff, all right? Here you go, Dr. Glenn."

"Ah, perfect. Thank you, Nurse."

Nurse? Gaia had to open her eyes no matter how much they were fighting her. What the hell was going on this morning? *Forget the blinding light, just push them. Push those lids open.*

Slowly but surely, Gaia managed to crack open her eyes and adjust them to the bright lights in the room. *Way too much white.* White walls, white lights, white sheets, and white coats. . .

"All right, folks, we lift on three. And one, two. . ."

Gaia felt her entire body lurch upward. Someone was lifting her. No, a few people were lifting her.

"Very nice. Just a few more details and we're good to go."

"Wait a minute," Gaia uttered, shaking her head from side to side, trying to shake off the thick veil of sleep. "Where am I?"

"Ah, I think she's finally coming out of it," a man said as his face leaned over her and smiled. The face was much too close. Everything suddenly felt much too

163

close. "Good *morning*, Gaia," he announced jovially. His voice was so loud and overexcited, it felt like he was calling a baseball game in her face. "*Great news.* Looks like you're well enough to be moved back to the medical facilities back home, so sit tight and we'll have you back in no time, all right?"

"Wait. What are you talking about?" She was positive she wasn't dreaming. But if this was real life, shouldn't *something* have made sense by now?

Finally the rest of her memories came flooding through. She remembered midnight snacks on the roof. She remembered falling asleep in Heather's room. But that was it.

Finally her vision was clear enough to see all the details. She was still in Heather's hospital room, but now it was bustling with nurses and orderlies, and they were all hovering around this one doctor. Doctor Glenn.

Heather. Find Heather. She flipped her head to the side to check on Heather.

Heather was gone.

"Where is she?" Gaia groaned, forcing out more and more volume as her eyes darted from stranger to stranger. "Where is Heather? What did you do with Heather?"

"Well, of course Heather's coming home, too," Dr. Glenn said.

"Who *are* you?" Gaia barked, locking her furious eyes with the doctor's.

"Oh, Gaia." He smiled, waving his finger at her. "Let's not play *that* game again, all right?" He turned and signed off on a few more pieces of paperwork from the nurses and then made not-so-subtle eye contact with a few of the orderlies. "The straps are secured?" he muttered nonchalantly.

"Secured, Doctor."

"Good. Well, then, let's get this patient back home, shall we?"

Straps? She'd been so disoriented and groggy, so obsessed with figuring out what was happening here—where Heather was, what on earth everyone was talking about—she hadn't looked down.

She hadn't been able to move her arm when she woke up because it was securely strapped to the mobile bed she was now lying on. Both arms were strapped down. And her clothes were gone. Someone had put her into a hospital gown. No, not *someone.* Dr. Glenn.

"Who the *hell* are you?" Gaia screamed. "Get these things off me *now*." She began to appeal urgently to the nurses and orderlies. "I'm not sick. This man is *not* my doctor. This is a trick. Get these goddamn straps off me!"

"I'm sorry," Dr. Glenn said to the nurses. "I was hoping she wouldn't disrupt the hospital. I'll have her out as quickly as I can. Like I said. . . a bit too rebellious for her own good. This is why I wanted the straps."

"It's quite all right, Doctor," the nurse replied with a pleasant smile. "I've seen much worse than this—"

"Listen to me!" Gaia howled. "I am *not* even a patient here. I was here visiting Heather Gannis. *Where* is Heather Gannis? Where are my clothes? Just take these straps off and I'll explain everything."

"All right, let's get moving," Dr. Glenn said, signaling the orderlies to push Gaia out the door.

"No! No, listen to me, goddamn it!"

"Yes, all right, Gaia." The doctor smiled condescendingly. "We'll have plenty of time to talk back home."

"Doctor," the nurse said, "I'm really sorry for that mix-up. I'll talk to the night nurse this evening. I don't know how we could have misplaced her chart."

"Not a problem," the doctor assured her as he led Gaia's stretcher out of the room. "I know all about glitches in paperwork. I'll have my assistant fax you copies."

"You asshole!" Gaia screamed. "Where's Heather? Where the hell is Heather?"

The moment they were out the door, the orderlies began to pick up speed. Dr. Glenn led them toward the elevator. Gaia pushed with every ounce of her strength to break free from the straps, but it was impossible. And the screaming only made her look like a raving psychopath. So she tugged. Again and again. She strained her aching wrists and biceps, clenched her teeth, and kept tugging with complete futility, watching helplessly as the ceiling rolled by in a blur.

ED SKATED WEST ON TWELFTH STREET.

Five Minutes

He'd sworn off all stunts for the rest of his life, but the board still made for some of the finest urban transportation in New York City.

He checked his watch. 9:50. *Perfect.* He'd make it to the hospital in five minutes and have enough time to check in on Heather and Gaia and still make it to school with three minutes to spare before Spanish.

He had the distinct feeling that everything was going to be a little brighter today. Maybe Gaia's uncle had just up and died in his sleep last night? Maybe Heather would have a little breakthrough with her sight? Why not? Why shouldn't things finally be a little less dark and painful for a change?

So Ed went ahead and convinced himself. He could do that now. He simply convinced himself that Gaia's uncle had given up and headed off to Greenland to retire. He convinced himself that Heather would be a little better when he walked into her room. Mind over matter. That's all it took. Even if Heather wasn't quite there yet, that wouldn't be a problem. Ed had enough optimism for both of them right now. Because he was only five minutes away now.

Five minutes to his fifteen minutes with Gaia.

Oh, come on, Ed. Fifteen minutes? You call that optimistic?

Right. He could be a little less conservative today. . . .
Five minutes to the rest of his life with Gaia.

THINK, GAIA. THINK. HOW DO YOU KILL

someone when you can't move? That
was one of the only two thoughts in
her head. How could she kill Dr. Glenn
without moving? And what had they
done with Heather? Gaia had sworn to
herself that she'd protect her, and it
was fast becoming another dead
promise in her life.

Poked
in the
Back

The orderlies seemed to be taking
pleasure in it. Who was she kidding,
they probably weren't even orderlies. Just more of
Loki's idiot thugs. That's what they were. And they
were enjoying it. They were practically grinning as
they watched Gaia writhing around furiously in the
straps, her limbs turning purple from the incessant
strain and the lack of circulation.

I swear to God, when I break out of these things. . .
whenever someone is stupid enough to unfasten these straps,
I'm going to rip those smiles off all your faces. Literally.

Dr. Glenn looked a hell of a lot more nervous now as
he scanned back and forth across the ambulance lot

every two seconds. Being a doctor was clearly his forte. The actual kidnapping part was another story. "Come *on*," he said, jerking his hand at the orderlies and guiding them toward a wide ambulatory truck that was parked out on the street just beyond the hospital's ambulances.

For one second, Gaia was out in the open air on Seventh Avenue, just two feet from hundreds of New Yorkers with their beautifully banal lives—rushing with their five-dollar coffees and their *New York Times*es, leaving their normal wives and lovers, walking their normal dogs, going to their normal jobs. Gaia had never envied them so much in her life. Strapped to a hospital gurney, being shoved along to who knew what fate. So pathetically helpless that all she could do was scream. Scream at those normal sons of bitches and beg for their help—beg for someone on the street to be intelligent enough to realize that doctors didn't roll patients along the goddamn *bike* lane of Seventh Avenue.

Wake up, she wanted to scream. *Can anyone see that something isn't right with this picture?* Of course not. The hospital's own *nurses* couldn't even put two and two together.

Ten more seconds and Gaia's little visit with the real world had ended.

The doors of the truck flew open, and Gaia cocked her head forward to get a good look. She honestly could not believe what she saw.

She'd known he was behind the whole maneuver;

she just hadn't expected to see, well. . . *him.* Not yet. But there he was, sitting right there in the truck. Loki in the center. And a Josh on either side of him. It was such a surreal image that Gaia even stopped thrashing around just to take it all in. All her enemies, gathered together. Shoulder to shoulder. Waiting for her.

The orderlies lifted her up into the truck and slid her in. And lying next to her was the answer to at least one of her questions. Heather. Still breathing, but unconscious on the gurney next to hers. Gaia turned back to her uncle (her father?).

And now that she was closer, she realized that the image was even more surreal than it had been at first.

There was something wrong with his face. His face and his body. His mouth kept twitching on the right side, repeating the same sick little half smile over and over, as if someone had filmed his face for three seconds and then looped the tape to repeat endlessly. His left shoulder had the same disturbing pattern—jutting upward every few seconds as if he were being poked in the back with an electric prod. And then there were his eyes. Stretching wide open and then blinking in two or three rapid flutters at a time.

They hadn't even closed the door to the ambulance, but ten good seconds of staring at Loki's (it was definitely Loki) maniacal face and Gaia was already getting motion sickness.

"What the hell is the matter with your face?" she asked,

trying to decide if she could bear looking him in the eyes while his face continued its unwatchable workout.

His shaking hand pulled a bottle of pills from his coat pocket, which he struggled to open. He slapped two of the pills into his mouth and then shoved the bottle back in his coat. And then he smiled. If you could call it a smile.

"I know you're none too pleased to see me," he said. "But that no longer bothers me, Gaia."

"How nice for you."

"Oh, if you only knew how nice."

Gaia quickly eyed the faces of the two Joshes on either side of him. It was strange. One of them looked quite vindictively pleased to see Gaia strapped down and completely at their mercy. That was, of course, what she would have expected. But the other. . . he looked oddly dissatisfied and sour. In fact, he wasn't even looking at Gaia. His eyes didn't stray once from Heather.

"It's really a shame that you hate me so much," Loki went on. "Especially now that we have so much in common, you and I."

"I have no idea what you're talking about."

"Yes, well, I'll explain it all a bit later. When we have some more privacy. For now, why don't you get some sleep. Dr. Glenn," he called out of the truck. "Shall we?"

Sleep? What did he mean, sleep? She'd just finally gotten up.

171

Dr. Glenn stepped into the truck, tapping a syringe to be sure it was clear of air. He leaned down toward Gaia.

"*No!*" she howled, writhing madly in her straps again. "No!"

But she knew her protests were useless. The doctor injected her at will. And within a few more seconds, it was all fading to white. Loki's repellent, jittery face finally disappeared from view.

EMPTY.

Tom's body went temporarily numb. He glimpsed his watch. 9:55. Whoever had sent him that memo had *promised* him Gaia would still be in Heather's room at *ten. Ten,* he'd said. Which had given Tom only thirty minutes to get all the way downtown. Tom had done it in twenty-five. So why was Heather's room empty? Where the hell was Heather Gannis? Where the hell was Gaia? Had Tom been crazy to take that anonymous tip seriously?

He was pounding on the window of the nurses' station before he'd even finished that thought. Why waste time thinking that question when he needed to be screaming it at one of the nurses?

172

The nurse jumped in her chair as Tom's fist nearly punched a hole in the Plexiglas wall of the nurses' station. He continued pounding until she stumbled out into the center of the hallway.

"*Excuse me, sir,*" she squawked, staring at Tom like he was an escaped schizophrenic from one of the other floors. "*Excuse me,* but this is a *hospital*—"

"Where is Heather Gannis?" Tom demanded. "She was in room 305 just last night. And my daughter was supposed to be visiting her. Where is my *daughter?*"

"Sir, if you would just calm down for a minute—"

"*Where is my daughter?*" Tom barked. "You've got ten seconds to tell me where she is."

"Are you a member of the family—?"

"*Yes,*" Tom snapped. "I'm counting down from ten. Ten, nine—"

"All right, all right," she squeaked. "I only asked because I assumed you knew. Ms. Gannis is being taken to her private medical facility back home."

"Her *what?*"

"Yes. They just took her downstairs to the ambulatory truck. Ms. Gannis and her sister, Ms. Moore."

Tom felt both of his lungs collapse.

"Ms. Moore?"

"Yes," she said. "Don't worry. Her private physician was here. Dr. Glenn oversaw the entire transfer. He's taking them both home for treatment, and I just assumed if you were a relative that—sir? Sir?"

Her voice disappeared in the background as Tom jumped entire flights of stairs to get back down to that street.

Her sister? What on earth went on in this hospital? The door, Tom. Just get to the door.

Tom snapped open his Blackberry and called for backup as he sprinted through the hospital lobby. But that call was utterly useless. Backup could take as much as twenty minutes. If he had any chance whatsoever, it would be gone in the next three. He drew his gun and burst out of the lobby, scanning Seventh Avenue from left to right.

And then he saw it. *The truck.* An ambulatory truck with a doctor stepping up inside. *In the middle of Seventh Avenue.* This was completely wrong. This wasn't where the ambulances loaded the patients. They didn't cart them out on the sidewalk before lifting them inside. And since when did the hospital's doctors hop into the ambulance for the trip?

Move, Tom. Move now.

He was already running.

"Gaia!" he shouted. But there was no response. He thrust his gun forward and ran for the ambulance. And as he got a few steps closer. . . he saw him. He could only see an off-balance glimpse, but he swore he'd seen *all* of them, in fact. Every single person in the world that he'd been trying to find for the last month, in the back of the same ambulance. His daughter, and Heather, and that son of a bitch kid who'd tried to kill Tatiana. . .

And finally his demented brother had revealed himself. Finally Tom's gun was where it had needed to be for the past month—maybe even the past twenty years.

Aimed at his brother's head.

But as he closed in with the gun, Tom could have sworn that his brother's only reaction. . . was to smile. He smiled the strangest, most inexplicable smile at Tom, and then he slowly disappeared from sight as his men began to close the back doors to the ambulance.

No. He won't just slip away. Not this time. Not again.

Tom knew he had only one chance. He was close enough. There was still enough room between the closing doors. He could jump it. He was sure. One well-planted leap and he'd be inside that ambulance, with a gun to Loki's head. . . .

As If

ED TOOK A SHARP TURN ON THE corner of Twelfth Street and zipped onto Seventh Avenue right at the entrance to St. Vincent's. He was rolling for the front door when he saw it. Not it. *Him.* He saw *him.*

It was one of those moments when the world suddenly spins at half its speed.

The wheels of Ed's board seemed to break down into a slow-motion roll as the entire horrid scene unfolded before his eyes.

Gaia's uncle. Running down the block with a gun. Running toward an ambulance.

Thoughts blasted in and out of Ed's mind at hyperspeed as he kicked his board up onto the sidewalk. Was Heather in that ambulance? Was Gaia? Was Gaia's uncle back just to finish the job on both of them? And then Ed remembered. He remembered what he had sworn to himself after seeing Heather lying in that hospital bed, after realizing that this was the man who'd sent out an order to have Ed shot. He swore that if he ever saw Gaia's uncle again, he would kill him. Or if not kill him, then at least put him out of commission for a long, long time.

And so, without even thinking, Ed poured on as much speed as he could pull out of his board and crouched down as low as he could get.

Aim for the legs, Ed. Out of commission. That's the goal. . . .

It was a full-on collision. Full powered. Fully fueled. Loud and painful and totally disconcerting. Gaia's uncle flew off his feet. His gun went tumbling onto the asphalt, and then they both followed, landing in a painful two-man pileup on the ground. Ed's face skidded against the rugged sidewalk. He could just barely hear her uncle screaming.

"*No*," he howled. Just "no." That was all Ed heard before her uncle rolled across the sidewalk and smashed into the side of the building. There were other sounds in all the chaos. He heard the doors of that ambulance shutting. He heard the screech of the tires as the ambulance took off down Seventh like a rocket.

If you were in there, then you're safe now, Heather. You're safe.

But Ed wasn't done. The human collision had brought something out of him. It had brought out all the anger. Anger he didn't even know he had. This was the man who'd tried to kill him. *Kill.* Not just hurt him. Not just scare him. *Kill* him. As if he had the right to do that. As if he had the right to decide who lived or died.

Ed was up on his feet before he knew it, and he was charging at Gaia's uncle, who was still on the ground. All his rage was channeled into his legs as he began to kick and kick without the slightest concern for what or where he was kicking. He just kept pounding away.

"You sick twisted *ass*hole," he spat, practically vomiting out every word from deep down in his gut. "Try to have me freakin' *killed*? What are you trying to do to us? Heather and Gaia and Tatiana and anyone else you can get your hands on. What kind of an uncle are you?"

"No," the man growled again from the ground. "No, you don't—"

"What kind of an uncle does that to his own *family*?"

177

Ed went on. He couldn't stop himself now. Nothing could stop him now. "Who *are* you? What kind of a sick—"

"*No, you idiot!*"

Suddenly Gaia's uncle took a swipe at Ed's legs, dropping him straight back down to the pavement. Before Ed could reorient himself, he felt the most agonizing pain he'd ever felt in his life, shooting through his neck and his spine, all the way down through his already weakened legs. It was some kind of torturous half nelson that left him completely contorted, driving the side of his face into the sidewalk.

"Enough!" her uncle screamed, grinding Ed to the ground with more and more pressure. "You *idiot!* You stupid, stupid *child!* I swear to God, I should break your idiot neck! I should just crack your—no, damn it. . . *Damn it. . . .*" He took a long, deep breath and blew it out. "I am *not* Gaia's uncle, Ed. I am her *father.* Her *father,* Ed. Her *uncle* was the man in that ambulance, along with my daughter and Heather Gannis. The ambulance that is now speeding off to God knows where." He finally released Ed from his torture.

Ed collapsed to the ground and stayed there, trying to regain the feeling in his entire body. But he wasn't sure he would ever want to get up again. Because he knew the man was telling the truth. He knew that this was in fact Gaia's father and that he had just made quite possibly the biggest mistake of his life. "I. . . I'm so. . . sorry. I thought—"

"No," her father interrupted, jumping up off the ground and then lifting Ed quickly and powerfully back to his feet. "There's no *time* for that," he barked, running a few steps ahead and swiping up his gun. "It was a *mistake*. That's all." He double-checked that his gun was still fully loaded as he began backing quickly toward his car. "You were trying to be noble, and you made a mistake. I know all about that, Ed. So just put it out of your mind and move on. Because I need your help now."

"Yeah," Ed said desperately, still reeling from the guilt in spite of her father's words. "So what can I do? How can I help?"

"You get up to the Seventy-second Street apartment and tell Natasha and Tatiana that Loki has Gaia and that I'm going after her. I want you to stay there. You stay there and you protect them, you understand?"

"I understand," Ed said.

"Go," Gaia's father said one last time. He ripped open the door to his car and started shouting urgent orders into his phone. "I need air support. Anything we've got in the area. We've got a white ambulance, thick red stripes on the sides and roof, headed south on Seventh Avenue. We must track this vehicle. We *cannot* lose this vehicle, copy? I'm in pursuit, but there have been delays here. . . ."

That was the last Ed could hear as Gaia's father slammed his car door and took off down Seventh Avenue, racing to catch up with the ambulance.

Delays, Ed thought, slapping his hands over his

head in shock and disgust, discovering all-new giant untapped wells of shame and guilt. *I'm the "delays." I'm the goddamned idiot of the century.*

Ed spun around three times before he even knew what direction he was going. He kicked his board up into his hand and ran for the subway uptown. He couldn't remember ever having despised himself more. He kept trying to remind himself of Gaia's father's words. They were so true. Ed had just been trying to be noble. And he'd made a mistake. A simple mistake.

But no matter how many times he told himself that, the same thoughts kept echoing over and over for the entire train ride up to Seventy-second Street and for every minute after that.

He has Gaia and Heather. He has them both. And I let him get away. No, I didn't just let him get away...

I helped him get away.

With the exception, perhaps, of pictures of Charles **trigger—** Manson, Gaia had **happy** never seen more clear-cut insanity in a man's eyes.

KEEP YOUR EYES OPEN. GAIA WAS finally awake enough to know how important it was for her to keep her eyes open. If she didn't keep them open, then she wouldn't be able to see the key details. She wouldn't be able to see who was being assaulted with Loki's

Too
Hideous

maniacal shouting. Much more important, she wouldn't be able to see what had happened to Heather.

That was the most infuriating part of being drugged again in that ambulance. Aside from the agonizing sense of helplessness, she knew that it also meant losing track of Heather. She couldn't guard Heather if she wasn't awake.

You've already missed enough. You must keep your eyes open.

But once she stretched open her crusty eyelids, she almost wished she hadn't. The image before her was so stark and ugly. And above all, *sad*.

Heather was strapped into a chair directly across from her. Her head was sagging off to the side, her eyelids half open and her lips parted, with an ugly white crust gathered at the dry corners of her mouth. There was no longer a trace of blood in her pale skin. The circles under her eyes were black. And after all the progress she had made the night before.

"Heather. . . ," Gaia whispered. "Heather, can you hear me? Are you okay?"

Answer me. . . . Come on, Heather, say something. Please. . .

"Gaia?" Heather whimpered. Her hands jolted into contorted positions under the straps and then settled again. She was still a mess physically, but she was alive. Gaia hadn't failed her completely just yet.

Heather's head darted up like a wounded animal's, veering off in all directions, trying to locate Gaia. Tears instantly fell from her vacant eyes. "Gaia, I thought I was alone. I thought I was going to die alone here."

"We're not going to die," Gaia stated plainly.

The truth was, the girl had more fight in her than Gaia would have ever imagined. Her survival instinct was yet another shot of inspiration. It had given Gaia the slap in the face she needed to shake off the rest of her grogginess.

She was thinking clearly now. She was assessing the situation. She checked her own stiff limbs, which Loki had of course strapped to her chair as well. She wanted to see if she could locate any slack in the straps this time. But there was nothing. Not a stitch of room to move or maneuver.

"Gaia," Heather whispered. "Is that your uncle screaming?"

"Yes."

"What's going on?"

"I have no idea," Gaia replied. She shifted her attention to her surroundings, examining the bare room around her as she tried to locate the origin of her uncle's incessant shouting.

The room was yet another indication that Loki had stepped way off the deep end. Gaia knew him. She knew how he'd always cared for the finer things, even if he was never excessive. When he took an apartment, it was always some spacious loft on some posh block in Chelsea or TriBeCa. Even the last time he'd managed to contain her, he'd kept her in some room filled with antiques and objets d'art and fine wooden furniture. But this place...

This place was an absolute dump. The floors were crumbling—probably from a termite infestation. The walls were only half painted. There were even big gaping holes and dents in the cheap drywall. There was basically no furniture—just the two chairs holding Gaia and Heather, another chair by the filthy windows, and a foldout table that was buckling from the giant crack at its center. Gaia ducked her head out the windows to see the entirety of the world outside, and she could see immediately that they weren't even in Manhattan. When you could see over the roof of every four-story building for miles, you knew you weren't in Manhattan. It was most likely Brooklyn. Maybe the Bronx. It was all so completely unlike Loki.

But it was easy enough for Gaia to do the math. She

and Heather were strapped to chairs. He'd already tried to burn Gaia and Tatiana to a crisp. His only mistake there: leaving them the use of their feet so that they could escape. He'd made the necessary adjustment now, simple as it might have been. He'd eliminated potential escape from the scenario. At least, that was probably what he thought. Gaia was still working on it. Though she had to admit... it wasn't looking good.

Conclusion: He'd had no need for a pricey loft downtown—no need to fill this crap-hole with outrageously priced antiques. Because he wasn't planning to stay for very long. Just long enough to finish what he'd started.

Gaia twisted her head far enough behind her to see them. She could see Josh sitting in the far corner of the room... or was it Josh? It might very well be QR1. Gaia had noticed in both the hospital and the ambulance that QR1 seemed to have lost the patented Josh smile. And he seemed to be brooding over something or thinking something through.

Once she managed to turn her head to its absolute limit, she could finally see where all the shouting was coming from.

Loki and Dr. Glenn were face-to-face, and Loki was barking at the doctor like some enraged army general chastising his pathetic new recruit. With the exception, perhaps, of pictures of Charles Manson, Gaia had never seen more clear-cut insanity in a man's eyes.

"If you utter another word about that stupid counter-agent," Loki shouted, "I swear to you, I will take this gun from my pocket, place it down the center of your throat, and empty the damn *chamber*. Not another *word*."

Counteragent. She'd still never gotten a straight answer from Heather. *Was there a counteragent?* Was there an antidote to the drug they'd given her? But hearing that word fall from Loki's lips set off a whole other chain reaction of thoughts. Thoughts that culminated in one very simple equation of images.

Gaia's eyes drifted back over to Heather's hands. She watched as they jolted from side to side under the straps, contorting violently for a half second and then lying completely still again. And then Gaia turned back to Loki's hands.

His left hand was shaking like an instant replay of Heather's.

Gaia might be jumping to conclusions, but she didn't think so. *He took it, too. He took the drug. He took his own demented fearless serum.*

That explained everything. The strange new twists in his body and his character suddenly made perfect sense. *Side effects.* Just like Heather. Loki had turned himself into a walking side effect. But if he'd injected himself with the same drug, then why were his tremors so much worse than Heather's? And more important, why couldn't *he* be the one who went blind?

Of course, none if those questions was the most important. The question in Gaia's mind now superseded all others. It was the same question she'd asked Heather in the hospital. Only now, judging from Loki's petulant screams at Dr. Glenn, she thought there was an answer to that question.

Was there a counteragent for the drug that was slowly killing Heather? Yes. Apparently there was, and Dr. Glenn was pushing Loki to take it. So where the hell was it? And how was Gaia going to get her hands on it? Especially considering the fact that she couldn't even move her hands.

She looked back at Loki. He was so much worse now. So much worse than what she'd seen in her one waking moment in the ambulance. Now his entire body was riddled with the mild tremors and tics. His eyes, his shoulders, his arms, everything was shaking on and off. Except for his right arm. His right arm was no longer shaking at all but was now as stiff as a petrified rock and tucked to his chest as if it were in a sling. He reached carefully into his coat with his left hand and pulled out that bottle of pills again.

"Do you really think those are *helping* you?" the doctor squawked. "Look at you. It's progressing even faster than I thought. Look at your arm. It's already in the next stage of—"

"Shut your mouth!" Loki hollered, shoving his trembling face closer to the doctor's. He carefully brought the jar of pills up to his mouth and ripped off the cap with his teeth. He tried to pour a few pills into his mouth, but a quick tremor of his arm sent the entire bottle of pills flying from his hand, falling onto the floor as the pills rolled out into every little decrepit nook and cranny of the dried-up wood. "Now look what you've done! Never mind. I don't need them. They're just hampering my transformation."

Loki's eyes drifted slightly, and he suddenly caught a glimpse of Gaia watching him. His eyes widened with excitement when he saw her. "Ah, you're awake. Good. Good."

He shoved the doctor out of his way and approached Gaia in her chair. Gaia's entire body stiffened as he stepped within striking distance. Or rather, it would have been striking distance if she had been at all able to strike. Instead she could only stare. She shot daggers and cannonballs and arrows and A-bombs at him with her eyes. But in the end, it was still only staring. Trembling or not, Loki was still in complete control.

"Yes, I know," he said, kneeling down so that he and Gaia were face-to-face. "You despise me. You'd love nothing more than to see me dead. You're probably thinking about how you'd do it right now."

A swift kick right to your windpipe. Untie me and I'll give you a demonstration.

"Well, Gaia, you'll be happy to know that I've changed. I've had a few revelations since we last spoke."

"You injected yourself with the drug, didn't you?" she asked him point-blank.

His eyes widened with surprise and perhaps even a little admiration. "You would have made a fine agent, Gaia," he said as his eyes fluttered open and shut and his shoulders twitched. His use of the past tense wasn't at all comforting. "Yes, you're right," he said. "I've put a piece of you back into me now. And now we're more similar than we ever would have been as father and daughter." Gaia cringed again at the thought of it. With each word his eyes seemed to burn brighter and brighter with that disturbing maniacal glow. Not to mention the exponentially increasing tremors that were making him too hideous and demonic to look at. "You see, we're finally the *same*, Gaia. All this time you've been able to look me in the eye and wish me dead. I'm sure you've wished it countless times, haven't you? You've been more than ready for me to just disappear off the face of the earth permanently. Your own father. Well, Gaia, it's taken me a long, long while, but now *I* am ready. That is the entire point of today. Because today... I am ready for *you* to disappear."

He reached his trembling hand into his coat pocket and slowly removed his gun. With Gaia unable to move or retaliate, he could take as much time as he needed. But that might have been too long.

The explosive thud at the door was so loud, even Heather knew where to turn. All heads turned toward the doorway just in time to see the shoddy front door of the apartment kicked in. Kicked *down,* actually. The entire door ripped from its rusty hinges and fell to the ground in a cloud of black dust.

And when he stepped through the door with his gun thrust out in front of him, Gaia wasn't even surprised. She was supremely elated, and relieved, and overjoyed. . . but not surprised.

Because she had always known that her father was a survivor.

TOM KNEW THERE WAS NO TIME TO

wait for backup. Given the situation, he'd had absolutely no choice but to go in guns blazing. He'd counted himself down from three and tried to picture the worst-case scenario before breaking the door down.

Final Family Portrait

But there was no way he could have pictured this scene. Tatiana's assailant was standing at the back of the empty room with a man in a lab coat (Dr. Glenn, he was quite sure). Heather and Gaia were both tied to chairs—Heather looking like a bleached white ghost shivering in her seat and Gaia with Loki's gun dangling in her face. And then there was the matter of Loki's body. . .

The image of his brother was far more horrifying than anything Tom could have concocted in his own head. Loki's body had fallen prey to some kind of heinous condition. Some parts of his body were convulsing like those of a Parkinson's patient, and other parts looked positively catatonic. Was he diseased somehow? Was this some kind of deadly reaction to a drug? Whatever it was, it was such a tragically disturbing sight that even as Tom pointed the gun at his head, he actually remembered his real brother for a moment. Maybe it was just the palpable weakness in his shaking body—the reminder that he was in fact human and not just some monster alter ego that his real brother had morphed into twenty years ago.

But that brief sense of his humanity disappeared just as quickly as Tom looked deeper into his brother's eyes. Because despite all the painful-looking facial tics and tremors, somehow he was still managing to give Tom that same vindictive grin. It was the simple act of taking pleasure in other people's pain. That was the quality that reminded Tom of the truth about his brother: that he *was* in fact a monster. He'd been a monster for years. The only difference now was that he actually looked like one.

"Drop it!" Tom ordered, moving two steps farther into the room. "Untie those girls right now. *Right now! Do it!*"

Loki smiled and stepped away from Gaia, moving

instead toward Tom with his own gun at his side. "Tom! Well, I see you got my invitation. But I think you're extremely confused," he said with a slight chuckle, moving closer and closer until he'd practically placed the front of his forehead against Tom's gun. "You seem to be under the impression that I can be scared by your gun. And I find that extremely ridiculous, since I'm no longer afraid of anything."

Tom was at a loss here. A complete loss. And Loki had obviously been counting on it.

"Drop it," a voice came from behind. Tom felt the barrel of a gun press firmly against the back of his head.

Invitation, he'd said. *I see you got my invitation. . . .*

Loki had sent the memo. This had all been planned. Of course it had all been planned. It was Loki. He'd *wanted* Tom to spot them escaping just so he would follow them, in this exact rush, without any time to gather backup. Just so he would rush by the thug who was waiting for him in the hall. Waiting for him to walk by so he could move in from behind for the ambush.

Tom raised his hands as an act of surrender, but he wouldn't drop the gun. Not yet. He wasn't prepared to do that yet. He turned his head just slightly to get a look at the man responsible for the ambush.

Wait. . . no, Tom assured himself. *There's no way he could have raced around from the back of the room. . . .*

Tom looked ahead of him again. He was *still there*

at the back of the room. The boy from the fire escape. The boy who'd tried to kill Tatiana. The boy Tom had seen shot in the head. This same boy was standing in front of Tom *and* behind him.

Twins? Had Loki hired twins? Some kind of sick homage to what he and Tom had lost as brothers? But what about the one Tom had seen get shot? Had there been *three* of them?

"I said, *drop it*," the boy repeated, jabbing his gun against Tom's head again. If Tom had had an extra half hour or so, he probably could have figured out the answer to this confounding puzzle, but with the gun still pressed to the back of his head, it wasn't going to take top priority. Top and only priority was to get Gaia and Heather out of there alive. And Tom certainly couldn't do that if he were dead. So he did finally drop the gun to the floor. The boy quickly grabbed Tom's arm and tugged it painfully behind his back.

Loki gave him another disturbingly volcanic version of a smile. "Yes, you always were on time, Tom. Like clockwork. Thank you for being so reliable. You're just in time for your execution. But don't worry, you won't be alone." He smiled again—or was it just another hideous twitch? And then he turned away.

Tom had certainly witnessed dementia in his brother's behavior before, but this was something else. This was ten times anything he'd ever seen before. This was a total psychotic break. Something or someone had flipped Loki all the way over the edge, and now he seemed to be just. . . free falling. Mentally and physically. And Tom knew how his brother's mind worked. If Loki were free falling, then he was planning to take as many people as he could plummeting down with him. Especially Tom and Gaia. The remains of his family.

Tom kept his eyes locked on Gaia's. Whatever happened now, he needed to maintain nonverbal communication with his daughter. He knew that as long as she was strapped firmly into that chair, there was simply no move to be made. But if they could somehow find an opening, they'd need to be on their toes.

Loki walked slowly away from Tom and stopped right at Gaia's side. He put his jittery left arm around her, letting his gun dangle over her shoulder. "What do you think, Tom? A lovely family portrait, eh? A fearless father and his fearless daughter."

"What are you talking about?" Tom squawked. Loki had clearly moved on to pure nonsensical verbiage.

"What am I talking about?" Loki smiled. "Well, I just thought you might want to get a `final family portrait`, Tom. Because I'm about to end this pathetic excuse for a family once and for all." He lifted his gun and pressed it shakily against Gaia's temple. "Why do you think I invited you here? I just wanted you to witness this historic moment firsthand. Consider the amazing *purity* of this moment. Here is a girl who is not afraid to die. And a man who is not afraid to kill her."

GAIA COULD FEEL THE WEAKNESS IN

Dangling Carrot

Loki's hand. She could feel him straining just to keep the gun pressed to her head. The side effects were winning out, she was sure of it. She probably could have knocked his entire twitchy frame to the ground with a well-placed snap of her head.

But there were too many variables. Even if she could head-butt him to the ground, that would still leave QR2 enough time to blow her father's brains all over the rotting floor.

She was sure it was QR2 holding the gun to her dad's head. Either that or Josh himself. Even though she couldn't see his wrist to be sure, she could see it in the hideous matching sparkle of his white eyes and teeth. He was reveling in sadistic joy at the thought of blasting a hole through her father's cerebellum, whereas QR1 still seemed to be suffering from a dour-faced attack of dissatisfaction and frustration over on the other side of the room.

So how did they get out of this one? Gaia was at a pathetic loss for answers. It was like her most poorly played chess game ever. Instead of thinking ahead five or six positions, she was stuck in her chair, hopelessly racking her brains just to find another move. And so, from the looks of it, was her father. He was just as paralyzed as she was in this miserable stalemate. If he made a move on QR2, it would still leave Loki's trembling gun `enough time to blow Gaia's head open`.

Gaia could see it now, almost like she'd been given a glimpse of the very near future. One shot would lead to three shots, which would lead to ten. The air of the inevitable was creeping up fast. It wasn't fear she was feeling, and it wasn't dread. It was simply something she knew. Loki and his accomplice had gone way beyond `trigger-happy`. Someone was going to take a bullet here, and she could do nothing to stop it. She could do nothing now but listen to her uncle's insane, disjointed ranting as the barrel of his gun wavered from her temple to her cheek to her chin and back to her temple.

"I suppose all revelations are simple, aren't they, Tom?"

Her father could only stare coldly and take in every manic word.

"Yes," Loki went on, "yes, that is the *definition* of a revelation, I think. When one realizes how very *simple* it all is. And I *have*. I have had such a revelation. And I wanted to share it with you. I wanted you both to hear it, Tom. You *and* my daughter—"

"Oliver, you don't know what you're—"

"*No*, Tom!" Loki bellowed, knocking his shaking gun against Gaia's head. She clenched her teeth to weather the sting of her vibrating skull. "Now you *listen*. You don't *speak* now, Tom! You're going to want to hear this. You're going to want to understand why you're both dying today—why we can *finally* put an end to this pointlessly drawn-out battle of twenty-odd wasted years. Don't you want to know, Tom? Don't you want to hear my revelation?"

Tom of course had no choice in the matter. Gaia watched as he bottled up every one of his real impulses and muttered his dishonest response. "Yes."

"*Yes,*" Loki hollered. "Yes, of course, you do. Well, here is the answer, Tom. Here is the truth that every one of us should have come to terms with long ago. My newfound lack of fear has shown me the way. I'll never know why you didn't come to this conclusion yourself long ago, Gaia, and kill *me,* as any enlightened person would have."

I'm working on it, Gaia thought, pointlessly checking her straps yet again for possible leeway. Another minute listening to his voice and she would have to do something very drastic. Something. *Anything* to shut his lunatic mouth.

"You see, all this time I've been the victim of one very simple and overwhelming fear," he said. "And *here* is the key. *Here* is the revelation, so pay attention: Our greatest fear in life is *not* what you think. Death. Death is *not* what we fear most in this world. Do you know what it is, Tom? Do you know what we fear most in this world? It is *loneliness.*"

His gun was battering her face with less and less control. Gaia could feel his hand on the brink of *something.* She couldn't tell if he was getting weaker by the moment or just more anxious to shoot.

"Yes. . . yes, loneliness. . . ," he went on, his voice quavering with intensity. "Having no *lover,* no companion. Having no *family,* no one on this planet who is a true reflection of you. That is what we fear. That is the equivalent of death to the average human being. That is what I have feared for all these years. And you see, that is why I am *free,* Tom. That is why all this foolishness can *end.*"

His entire body suddenly hunched over. Gaia saw her father inch forward, but Loki regained his balance, however shaky, and shoved the gun back into her cheekbone. QR2 plugged his gun more firmly into her father's head.

"*Don't you even. . . ,*" Loki warned. He was forcing out every word now. Pushing each consonant and vowel through his contorted lips and his bobbing head. "You're not *hearing me,* Tom. You're not paying attention. You see, I'm *not afraid* anymore. I'm not afraid to be alone. I am ready now. I'm ready to be completely self-contained, self-reliant, and self. . . *defined.* I am ready to accept. . . that my own flesh and blood *despises me.* Katia despised me. . . . You despise me. . . . Now *Gaia.* So, you see. . . I no longer need a family. I am ready to. . . *dispose* of my family. I am ready to say. . . good-bye."

He squeezed his trembling finger on the trigger,

and Gaia could swear she felt time freeze. It was as if time had added two seconds to this minute, granting Gaia one extra moment before her death. There would be no chaos, no panic. Her entire life wouldn't pass before her eyes as she'd always been told, but rather her thoughts would become simple and concise. And though she had wondered it many times, now she finally knew. Gaia finally knew what she would be thinking at her death. There would have been time for more, but in the last moment she found herself with only a few thoughts: (1) *Dad, I forgive you for all your mistakes, and I love you. When he shoots me, you make your move. You take him down and everyone else in this room. And bring Heather home.* (2) *Ed, the three words were* I love you. *I said them only once, but I loved you, Ed. I loved you like nothing I ever could have remotely understood or handled.* And (3) *Mom, Mary, Sam. . . I'll be there in a minute.*

Gaia locked her eyes with her father's one last time and then prepared for the sound of the gunshot. She would not flinch. She would not move in the slightest. And just as she had always known, her eyes would remain wide open. Until the end, and long after her death.

But the gunshot never came. Instead Loki fell quite suddenly to his knees.

He dropped down to the floor in a half-convulsive, half-paralytic heap. His hand stayed glued to his gun, but his arm had given in to a wild series of spasms. The sight was so horrific that Gaia could do nothing but stare. Her quick preparation for death fell away as the impulse to escape instantly replaced it, coursing through her body faster than adrenaline. But the unfortunate realities remained. She was still thoroughly immobile, and her father was still being held at gunpoint.

And then another voice was shouting instead of Loki's. A voice from across the room. The voice of Dr. Glenn.

"Do you see now?" he called out, staring down at Loki with a kind of desperate disapproval as he dug his hand deep into his lab coat pocket. "Do you understand that you *need* the counteragent? You need it *now*."

Gaia's eyes zoomed to the doctor's pocket. *He's got it. He's got the counteragent in his pocket. You need to get it. How the hell do you get it? Think.* But no amount of thinking would do a thing. The counteragent was across the room. It could have been six inches in front of her face, and it still wouldn't have mattered. It was a dangling carrot she could never reach.

"Shut *up*," Loki hissed, struggling to lift his decimated body off the ground. "You think these. . . harmless spasms frighten me? They mean *nothing* to me. *Nothing*."

"You *need* this injection to survive," the doctor shouted. "I don't care what you fear. Being fearless does not make you a fool—now, *take it*." The doctor dug farther into his pocket.

"You don't call me a fool!" Loki hollered, finally getting back to his knees as he tried to steady the arm that held the gun. "You don't issue orders or ultimatums, Doctor. You don't *talk* anymore. You shut your fearful, weakling, idiot mouth or I kill you first!"

"I'm trying to save your life," the doctor pleaded angrily. "Let me save your life, for God's sake. Complete paralysis is the next step. Complete paralysis and then *coma*. Now, if you would prefer to spend the rest of your life in a coma—"

"*Enough!*"

Gaia could barely hear Loki's scream over the booming echo of his gun. He fired off two thunderous shots at the doctor that reverberated through the empty room like a sawed-off shotgun. Heather screamed at the top of her lungs as she pulled her head deep within her shoulders and crushed her useless eyes closed from sheer reflex.

Somehow, despite his wild spasms, Loki had still found the strength to aim. Gaia watched as the first shot erupted in the doctor's shoulder, knocking him back against the wall. And then the second shot hit. It blew a black, bloody hole in the left side of his stomach.

The room became eerily quiet. Dr. Glenn stared wide-eyed at Loki, gazing in shock and disbelief at what he had just done. And then he began to fall, sliding slowly and painfully down to the floor, leaving a thick trail of blood down the ugly white wall.

"I can't. . . ," the doctor uttered quietly. "Why would you. . . ?" He seemed too shocked to complete a sentence as his breathing rapidly became more labored. He could no longer move, but he panned his eyes across the room, looking at the silent audience who could do nothing to prevent his death. And then the look in his eyes took one last shift. It shifted to something cruel and hateful.

"*Good*," the doctor stated, taking in only shallow quarter breaths as he fixed his eyes on Loki. "I'm the only one who could re-create that counteragent. I. . . told you this was the last vial. You've just signed your own death sentence, you idiot. You pathetic. . . ignorant. . . No—"

Loki fired off another flailing shot. It didn't even hit the doctor. It only left a black hole in the wall next to his head. But it didn't matter. The doctor had already died. His face fell to his shoulder as his arms sprawled out on the floor like an old rag doll's.

And Gaia could already see the thought pass over Loki's face. She could see him realize what he had just done. Finally he seemed to have discovered whatever remained of his rational mind.

He needed that counteragent. Of course he needed it. He needed it right now. And killing the doctor had left him with only one vial of it remaining. So he began to move, ever so slowly. He rose to his feet, still hunched over by his spasms and his paralysis, looking like some pathetic joke—looking like someone's horrible imitation of some operatic monster—the Hunchback, or Igor, or The Fly. It would have looked so fake if Gaia didn't know how very real it was. It would have been funny to stare at or so sad. . . if it weren't so disgustingly ugly.

"I don't want to see *anybody* move," he ordered, each word sounding awkward and twisted pouring from the corner of his contorted mouth.

He barely kept his gun aimed at Gaia's face as he backtracked step by step toward the doctor's corpse and crouched down next to him. He set down his gun and kept his eye on Gaia as he dug his usable hand into the doctor's lab coat pockets.

"Where is it?" he shouted, patting down the pockets again and again. Gaia could see his rage and desperation fast approaching the boiling point. *"Where the hell is that counteragent!"*

"It's right here." A voice echoed through the room. All heads turned to the source of that voice.

The once dour-faced QR1 was now proudly holding up the vial to Loki.

Gaia's heart sank to new depths. She had hoped

that perhaps the last vial might have been lost somewhere in that room, somewhere where they might
have found it after Loki had been subdued. Then she
could have given that last dose to Heather, who had
been growing grayer and more vegetative by the
minute. At the very least, Gaia had hoped that someone had destroyed it—that Loki would never see the
counteragent again and that he would succumb to
every symptom the doctor had predicted, falling into a
tragic state of complete paralysis and then a lifelong
coma.

But once again, the slightest bit of optimism
had been too much. QR1 had obviously been pro-
tecting the vial for Loki this entire time, being the
mindless thug that he was. He had simply been
holding it for safekeeping until the Grand High
Boss needed his medicine. Gaia was overcome by a
wave of utter hopelessness and nausea as she stared
at this pathetic excuse for a father-son team. The
test-tube slave saving his master's ass. How
thoroughly repellant.

Loki breathed out a desperate sigh of relief.
"Excellent," he said, holding his trembling arm out to
QR1. "Give me the shot. . . quickly."

Gaia did everything in her power to will that vial
out of QR1's hand as he stepped forward. If she could
just will that last vial to drop from his hand and crash
to the floor.

But it was no use. The vial stayed firmly in his grip. He stepped toward Loki and looked down at him.

And then he turned away.

He turned to his right, crouched down next to Heather Gannis, and gave her the shot.

Remnants of a Scream

"WHAT. . . WHAT ARE YOU DOING?" Loki cried.

Gaia was rather sure her jaw was still hanging open. As was her father's. As was QR2's. The entire room had been left dumbfounded and speechless. All of them with the same question. The same question Loki had just whimpered childishly from the floor. What was QR1 doing? *Why?* Why had he used the last vial on Heather and not Loki?

Gaia had never seen this look on Loki's face. Never. She had never seen his eyes without that veil of confidence and absolute power. She had never seen his brows arched in total shock, like a child who'd gotten lost in the woods or an old woman who'd just had her purse snatched. The epitome of helplessness.

All he could do was stare and watch it happen. Watch as QR1 injected Heather with the counteragent and then threw the empty vial down on the floor, breaking it into infinitesimal shards. Heather let out the remnants of a scream, but that was all. She was too weak to resist. And thank God for that. Her life had just been saved, and she probably didn't even know it.

"What are you doing?" Loki squawked again. "What the hell do you think you're *doing*?"

QR1 rose to his feet and walked slowly to Loki until he was towering over his gelatinous body on the floor. "I'll tell you what I'm doing, *sir*. I'm doing something you've never done in your entire life." He knelt closer. "I'm honoring my brother."

"*What?*" Loki raised his eyes up to his. "What are you *talking* about?"

"I'm talking about Josh," he spat. "My *brother*. My twin brother. The one you killed."

"Oh, please, he wasn't even your—"

"Shut *up*," QR1 shouted. "Yes, he *was*. He *was* my brother. We were all brothers, whether you ever understood it or not. And my brother wasn't an idiot. He knew his days were numbered. He could feel it. So he asked me. He made me promise that I would get Heather that counteragent if he couldn't to do it himself before he died—no, let me rephrase—before you *killed* him. And I promised. I swore to him that I'd get it done. And I did."

QR1 suddenly turned to Gaia. "I was *trying* to give

it to Heather in the hospital," he explained, "but they were watching me, and she was so nervous, and then *you* came barging in, Gaia. I *told* you that you didn't understand what was going on in there."

Gaia couldn't possibly have uttered a response at this moment. Nor did he seem to need one. He turned right back to Loki before she could have even opened her mouth.

"So that injection was for Josh," he proclaimed. "Not for you. Never again for you."

"That's enough," Loki hissed, trying clumsily to climb to his knees. "Not another word, you little—"

"No, I've got another word," he barked. "I've got plenty more words, *sir*."

"You're an experiment!" Loki growled. "A god-damned test case for an experiment that *failed*. I should have terminated *all* of you years ago—"

"I am just *so glad* that it's done!" QR1 howled, ignoring Loki entirely. Finally his patented smile had returned. Only now it was in an entirely different context. "I'm *so glad* that was the last of the counteragent and that you'll probably rot right here in this crappy torn-down apartment like an old petrified fossil. That's what you deserve. Not just for Josh, but for every other one of my brothers that you've killed without even thinking twice. You think we're nothing but experiments? You think *we're* less than human? Us? *You're* the subhuman here. You're less human than we will ever be. And now you're *done*. I hope once that coma kicks in, you never wake up."

Loki's eyes had glazed over by now. His expression had moved beyond rage or disbelief or spite into some strange blank netherworld. But Gaia knew exactly what his expression meant.

He had just had his final revelation. A revelation Gaia would have been happy to impart had she chosen to even dignify his `pseudophilosophical psycho ranting` with a response.

She knew next to nothing about fear, but she certainly knew this much: Yes, people fear death more than most things. And yes, they might fear loneliness even more. But the thing that people fear *most*. . . is the combination of the two. The thing that people fear most is dying alone. Which had always struck Gaia as extremely odd. Since everybody dies alone.

But of course, Loki had always placed himself above everybody else. He suffered from hubris to the nth degree. And he would never accept the notion of dying alone. Which must have been why he started shooting.

He thrust his convulsive arm forward and fired off his deafening gun again and again, waving it around wildly as he howled out a stream of indecipherable hatred. He clearly had no specific target in mind now. He just wanted to take them all down with him.

QR1 was the first to go. Gaia had barely had a chance to blink before his entire torso was covered in bullet holes. The sheer force of the shots forced him to shuffle backward three steps before collapsing to the ground. The chaos turned so ugly, Gaia almost wanted to shut her eyes. Not because she was afraid, but simply to avoid stocking up on more images for her nightmares. But chaos always moved too quickly to avoid.

QR2 swung his gun away from her dad and took his first step toward Loki to protect his brother, but it was already far too late to protect a corpse. He hadn't even finished the first step when Loki's wild bullet spray decimated his ankles, sending him to the ground as two more holes erupted in his head.

Move. Move now and move fast, Gaia ordered herself. *You are in the line of fire, wherever the hell that is.*

Gaia pushed off with her toe just to knock her chair over to the side. That was the only maneuver she had left. But as her chair tipped over, she saw him.

She saw her father covered in blood and falling to the floor headfirst.

TOM HAD TO MAKE A SPLIT SECOND

Irrational Reflex

decision. Seeing Gaia's chair tip over had made his heart stop. If she'd been hit, then his ability to live with himself would have finally reached its limit. But the only way to be sure no one got hit again—the only way to put an end to this thing—was to get to the source. Loki's gun.

With the twins, or whatever they were, dead on the floor, Tom knew he'd be next if he kept his feet to the ground. He had to jump. But which way? Over to Gaia to pull her out of the line of fire, or over to Loki to disarm him?

You know the answer, Tom. Get that gun out of his hand or you'll all be dead in five more seconds.

So he jumped headfirst, covered in his dead captor's blood, and prayed he could dodge the bullets for just one more second. . . .

"*Aaagh!*" Loki let out a high-pitched wail.

Tom ripped the gun from his frail hand and plowed his shoulder into his chest, rolling his brother flat against the floor as he cried out again. The sound gurgling up from Loki's chest was so painful and pathetic, Tom almost regretted tackling him so hard. But that was just an `irrational reflex`. He quickly reminded himself of the amount of pain his brother deserved—so much more than one man could inflict. More than an army could inflict. In fact, Loki deserved much worse than pain. Tom knew for a fact that nearly every system of justice, from that of the most primitive tribe to the most civilized country, would agree. . . .

Loki's crimes were punishable by death. It was more than justified.

Images were rapid-firing through Tom's head. Katia's dead body lying flat on the kitchen floor. Gaia lying on the floor right now, strapped to a chair like a prisoner of war.

Tom grabbed onto the front of his brother's shirt and hoisted his torso off the ground, pressing the barrel of the gun firmly to his forehead. If there had ever been a time to make an exception to his strict moral code, it was now. One simple gunshot to the head would finally ensure that this war was truly over—that Tom would never again have to look behind his back and wonder when the next murder attempt on his loved ones was coming.

He realized now that his tackle had put an end to Loki's convulsions. Loki had now given way completely to the paralysis, his neck frozen at a stiff thirty-degree angle, his right arm curled up against his side like an injured wing, and his left hand frozen in a clenched fist that clung to Tom's lapel. His eyes were no longer twitching, either. Now they were simply fixed on Tom's eyes in a hollow, impenetrable expression that bordered somewhere between pure hatred and animal desperation.

Neither of them uttered a word. Tom wasn't even sure Loki was capable of speech at this point. But it wouldn't have mattered. It wouldn't have mattered what either one of them said. It wouldn't have mattered what either one of them did next.

Tom wasn't going to pull the trigger, and he knew it.

Despite their supposedly identical DNA, Tom simply didn't have a vengeful gene in his body. Maybe his brother had taken Tom's in the womb. Maybe that explained why Loki seemed to have twice the need for vengeance of any other human being and Tom simply had none. He had certainly been pushed hard enough to question his need for vengeance. But here, with a gun pointed directly to his brother's head, was the answer. *No.* No, he couldn't kill his brother in cold blood. Even though Loki had been more than ready to do just that to him. That was really the point, though, wasn't it? Tom *wasn't* his brother. He wasn't Loki. And he never would be.

Besides, Tom didn't really need to exact revenge. Loki had somehow managed to bring his own worst fate on himself.

Tom lowered the gun from Loki's head and dropped his paralyzed torso back down to the floor. He turned and stepped quickly to Gaia.

"Are you hurt?" he asked, crouching urgently by her chair as he removed the tight straps from her hands and feet.

"I'm fine," she said. "Where are you hit? I can't see where you're hit."

"I'm not hit," he replied quickly. "This isn't my blood, Gaia. You get Heather."

Gaia quickly undid Heather's straps as Tom stepped back down to Loki on the floor. A moment more and he felt Gaia right behind his shoulder.

Tom peered into his brother's cold and help-less eyes, which were just about the only things he seemed capable of moving now. Tom was at a complete loss for what to do or say.

But much to his surprise, in spite of what looked like complete paralysis, Loki managed to reach his crippled left arm up and grab onto Tom's lapel again, pulling him closer with whatever was left of his strength.

Tom could hear him straining to speak through his phlegm-ridden gurgles and his iced-over face. He was definitely trying to say something. Something was changing now. . . . He was giving up. The harshness fell away from his eyes, leaving only that unwatchable air of childlike desperation.

"I can't understand you," Tom said, fighting off the sudden unwanted sympathy he was experiencing as he leaned closer. "Say it again."

Loki tightened his fist around Tom's lapel and tugged him even closer. He was still the man that Tom had always known—still using his iron will to fight off the obvious lack of consciousness that was approaching. That's how important it was for him to say whatever it was he had to say. And finally Tom was close enough to hear the strained words falling from Loki's locked jaw.

"My daughter. . . ," he moaned. "I want to see her."

Tom yanked back his head and stared into his brother's eyes.

Just a few minutes before he'd heard Oliver refer to

Gaia as his own daughter. But this was the first time Tom could see it so clearly. It *wasn't* some kind of psychological ploy or tactic. It wasn't some kind of conniving means of manipulation.

His brother honestly still didn't know. After seventeen years, he'd still never learned the truth.

"Oliver," Tom began, flashing his eyes to Gaia and then back to his brother. He could only think of him as Oliver now, lying on the floor in such a state. "Oliver, you still don't understand, do you? I just. . . assumed you had seen your tests at some point. . . ."

"What tests?" Loki whispered, slurring to try and hold words together.

"Your fertility tests," Tom said, once again struck by the irrational need to be gentle with the cruelest man he knew. "Oliver, you're completely sterile, don't you know that? You have been ever since that experimental treatment when you were thirteen. The tests. . . they're just sitting there in your Agency files, but I assumed. . . I assumed you knew by now."

Oliver's eyes seemed to be receding into his head. It was as if he were progressively shrinking from pain. Although it didn't look so much like pain in his eyes now. It looked like sadness. "What. . . you talking about?" he muttered, saliva building up in his permanently open mouth.

"What are you saying?" Gaia demanded from behind.

"I'm saying he's not your father." Tom locked eyes

with his daughter. He was shocked to see some kind of dark, oppressive burden suddenly fall away from Gaia's eyes. He hadn't even wanted to have this conversation in front of her, but from her look it seemed she somehow knew more than he or Katia had ever chosen to tell her. She seemed quite aware that there had at one time been the potential for Oliver to be her father. Yet the simple fact of his sterility had somehow been omitted. Until now.

Tom turned back to Oliver. "Gaia is not your daughter," he stated clearly and for the record. "You're incapable of having a daughter, Oliver. You never could have fathered a child, and you never will. You're incapable of—"

Tom stopped. He felt the need to stop. Because in spite of his brother's almost completely catatonic face, a tear was now falling from the corner of his eye and dripping down to the wooden floor.

And Tom felt so relieved. Oliver wasn't going to waste his time doubting what was obviously the truth. He knew Tom. He knew Tom wouldn't lie to him right now. He knew Tom had never once lied to him in their entire lives. Oliver had been told the truth, and he had accepted it.

His fist pulled tighter on Tom's lapel. It clenched down with such force that it turned bright white from the pressure as he pulled Tom even closer.

Tom could tell that Oliver had some version of last words to speak now. Something he urgently needed to say to his brother before he faded away. Most likely a plea for forgiveness for an `infinite list of merciless crimes`... and Tom was prepared to give it.

"What is it?" Tom replied. "I can still hear you." He leaned his ear to his brother's lips.

Oliver breathed his words into Tom's ear. "I hope... that you die like this, Tom. I hope that you die paralyzed, and alone... and loved by no one. I know that's how you'll die. And you'll be scared. So pathetically scared. But I'm not scared, Tom. I'm not afraid to die alone...."

Tom stared into his brother's very unenlightened eyes. "Then why won't you let go of me, Oliver? Why have you been pulling me closer and closer?"

Oliver had no answer for this. But his sudden attack of speechlessness spoke volumes. Apparently he intended to carry his denial with him all the way to the other side. He looked at Tom one last time. He shifted his watery eyes to gaze at Gaia. And then, with nothing left to say, he simply closed them. He closed his eyes for good.

It was over. The war was finally over.

"Is he dead?" Gaia asked.

Tom cracked open Oliver's eyes and peered through the pupils. "Comatose," he said. "Brain-dead. Vegetative state. He'll probably stay that way for years. Until his body finally rots away and his heart stops."

"That sounds worse than being dead."

"It is."

"Good," Gaia said, staring down at his nearly

lifeless body. "He deserves something worse. What do we do with him?"

"I don't suppose it really matters now," Tom said. "We'll wait here until the Agency picks him up. They'll lock him away in some medical facility. They'll probably want to run a lot of tests."

"So. . . he'll just be a test subject from now on?" Gaia asked.

"I suppose so."

Gaia shook her head and coughed out the remains of an ironic laugh.

"What?" Tom asked.

"Nothing," she said. "Never mind."

Tom raised his head and gazed across the room at all the pointless destruction. Dr. Glenn was sprawled out on the floor, his head still propped up against the drying streak of blood on the wall. The twin brothers were lying next to each other in a puddle of blood. And Oliver's body was lying before him in a lifeless heap.

But Heather Gannis was alive. Curled up and still only half conscious in her chair, but alive. And Gaia was alive. And Tom was alive. And the Agency would be arriving shortly. To clean up the mess.

Hold them at
bay while
the sun was
still **stunning**
out.
Before the **boy**
timer
started its
countdown
again.

I realized something ten minutes
ago. I realized it the moment I
stepped foot out the front door of
that decrepit Brooklyn brownstone
with Heather hanging her arm
around my shoulders and the sun
glaring so harshly in my eyes that
I felt nearly as blind as she was.

I lost track of all of it for a
second. I lost track of the swarm
of agents surrounding me, and the
body bags, and Loki's functionally
dead body being wheeled into an
Agency van, and even my father,
who I hadn't hugged yet in all the
insanity of the morning.

I lost track of everything but
the sunny urban wasteland surrounding me on all sides.
Somewhere in the deepest out-
skirts of Brooklyn. Completely
neglected by mankind probably
since at least the late 1970s.
Nothing but boarded-up brownstones, and abandoned rusty
Dumpsters, and gigantic Newport
cigarette billboards covered over
completely with graffiti.

And it looked to me like
heaven. Total and complete heaven.
The bright, vivid colors of the
graffiti, the reflection of the
golden sun in the rust of the
Dumpsters, the millions of glis-
tening specks of quartz in the old
sidewalks. . . It was my very
first sight of freedom.

Because that's what I realized
as I stepped foot out into that
heavenly wasteland.

I realized that I had been
raised in captivity.

Just like any ape in the zoo,
just like any cranky parrot in a
two-foot-high cage living in some
grandmother's dark apartment that
looks out on the air shaft.

Needless to say, the irony
didn't escape me. Here I'd been
under the impression that I was
probably the most independent
being on the planet—that every
choice in my life was entirely up
to me. But I was so wrong. I
didn't even realize how wrong
until ten minutes ago.

All my choices and all my family's

choices had really just been coping mechanisms to survive *him.* Whether we could see the actual cage or not, we had always been Loki's captives. Everything we'd done since I was six years old had been dictated by his existence. We'd moved to the Berkshires to run from him. My mother died because of him. My father abandoned me to protect me from him, which is what landed me in the care of George and Ella Niven (need I even say more about them?). I lost Sam because of him, I lost Mary because of him, and I nearly lost Ed for the same reason.

A *slave.* I've been a complete *slave* to his will—to his entire freaking existence. And to think I'd never even known it until this year. That's *ten years* of complete ignorance. Eleven of my most formative years lived in captivity. The better part of this year as more than just his captive but as his goddamned guinea pig—his fearless specimen.

And now *he'll* finally be the captive. If I've ever questioned the notion of karmic justice, I swear I'll never question it again. Because Loki is the captive now. A captive inside his own vegetative body for the rest of his quasi-life. And if enjoying that makes me cruel, then so be it, but I don't think he's lived a life deserving of one drop of respect. So I had to laugh. I had to laugh for at least a second when I realized what the future held for my uncle. My dad said they were probably going to run tests on him, maybe try to find out what had turned him into such a sadistic freak, and that seems just perfect to me. He's going to live out the rest of his nonlife flat on his back and as someone *else's* test subject for a change.

And now I'm actually free. Not my old definition of free. Not free as in escaping the reality of the situation. Not free as in free to beat on whoever I choose. But *actually* free. Free to pursue an actual life. Free to hope for all the things I'd sworn to avoid

for all eternity, like friends
and boyfriends and a *family.*

And while that's all quite undeniably heavenly, the truth is. . .
I have no idea how to do that. I
don't know a damn thing about freedom. I don't know a damn thing
about hope or optimism or creating
my own fate. I don't know how to
act. I only know how to *react.* For
a goddamned genius, I know next to
nothing about life outside a cage.

So what *do* I know?

I know that Loki isn't my
father, a fact which I will be
continuously celebrating for the
next twenty or so years. I know
that if I'd just had my real
father *around* more that I might
have learned this fact about Loki
much earlier and avoided a whole
crock of painful doubts and repul-
sion. In fact, I know that there's
probably a world of things my
father could have explained to me
if he hadn't lived so much of his
life as one of Loki's captives.

But I also know that my father
is back now. And he's going to be

here for a while. So I'll have time to ask every single question I should have been asking for the last ten years. And he'll have time to answer me.

I know that I need to see Ed Fargo as soon as possible and tell him that I'm planning on taking hours and hours of intensive girl-friend lessons. I need to explain to him that growing up alone in a cage leaves one with the exact same human-to-human skills as any other zoo animal or house pet. Ed must know something about that after those years in the chair. That chair must have been kind of like a cage at times. And the freedom to walk again must have felt a little like stepping onto the moon. But still, I don't think that's the same. Ed just had to relearn this whole freedom thing.

I, on the other hand, will be learning freedom from scratch. At an awfully late age.

Bear with me, Ed. *Please* just bear with me.

Insanely Storybook Moment

"I'D LIKE TO MAKE A TOAST IF I could...."

Gaia's father stood up from the table and raised his glass. But as he began to speak, his voice faded from Gaia's mind. She strained for the tenth time in the last half hour to accept the sight of her "new family" at this grand dining-room table as a truly untainted, non-dream-related, non-drug-induced reality.

It wasn't as if rationally she couldn't recognize that it was real. It was just that the whole scene was so frustratingly dreamlike, Gaia could barely find her place in it.

Everyone sitting around the dining table in this posh Upper East Side apartment; her father at the head of the table, smiling, with his glass raised; Natasha and Tatiana both unharmed and smiling comfortably; Ed sitting right next to her, quite possibly as in love with her as she was with him...

This moment was only supposed to exist in Gaia's embarrassingly childish fantasies. This was meant to be nothing more than a fictional archetypal image. One of those ridiculous and unattainable dreams that only served as beautiful fiction, keeping Gaia moving forward through the drudgery of her *real* life.

But it was all undeniably real. It had been real from the moment they'd dropped Heather safely back at the hospital and then walked through the door of the apartment. That's when Gaia had seen Natasha, sitting on the living-room couch, most definitely alive, just as Gaia had promised Tatiana she would be. Her arms were glued securely around Tatiana as if she had no intention of letting go for a number of days. And just a few feet from their magnetized embrace was Ed Fargo.

Ed had been sitting on the edge of the couch like a huge welcome-home gift with an intoxicating smile. All three of them had been waiting anxiously for Gaia and her father's safe return. And when Gaia and her father had walked through that door, the three of them smiled with such acute relief, it actually made Gaia want to let out a huge breath of her own, even though she hadn't been the least bit anxious.

Gaia had been trying since then to breathe in the reality here, but this moment at the dining table was still so. . .

Just listen to your dad, she told herself. *Listen to his toast and you'll settle in.*

She took her own advice and tuned back in to her father. But luckily she hadn't missed anything yet. He and Natasha were having a little domestic squabble over wine. Even their domestic squabble seemed too enchanting to be real. But it was. All of it was unmistakably real.

"Oh, come on, Tom." Natasha laughed. "You can't toast with a glass of water. Let me pour you a glass of wine."

"Water will do," he said with a smile.

"No, no," Natasha insisted, standing up from the table and stepping into the kitchen as she spoke. "Just a little in your glass for the toast, yes? That's all. I've been holding on to this one bottle for a special occasion, and I doubt very much there will *ever* be a more special occasion than all of us sitting here, together and alive at this table today."

"Well, I think you may be right about that," Tom replied. Gaia couldn't have agreed more. With all the secrets out of the way, Natasha was beginning to grow on her more and more by the minute.

Natasha stepped back to the dining table quickly and poured a little wine into one glass for Gaia's dad. She set the bottle aside on the desk and rushed back to her chair.

"Well, then," Tom went on. "A toast. . ."

Gaia took a few deep breaths and gazed at her father. Even though she'd known it for at least an hour now, this was the first time she had truly *felt* it, as she let herself focus in on him at the head of the table.

He was back. He was truly back. It was almost as if Gaia had spent these last hellacious months taking the father she'd always known and pulling him apart piece by piece, ripping him up into tiny jagged pieces and examining him from every possible angle before finally putting him all back together. But now that he had been fully reassembled in her heart, Gaia could finally look at him with her own eyes, instead of the eyes of a twelve-year-old. She knew that today was the day she had begun to admire him for the man he was. Not just the father.

"First and foremost," he said, "to my daughter." Gaia felt her heart jump into her throat. "Gaia, I am never leaving your side again," he said, staring comfortably into her eyes. "*Ever.* If it takes us ten years, I will make up for all the time that my brother ripped away from us." Gaia believed him. She felt herself blushing, though, and lowered her head slightly just to recover. Ed grabbed her hand under the table and squeezed it tightly. This, of course, only served to double the amount of blood rushing to her face. Her dad smiled a knowing smile and moved on.

"To Heather Gannis. She's safe and sound back at the hospital now, and the doctors have already seen some marked improvement in her health. She's shown clear signs that the sickness is reversing itself. Her doctor told me that with some hard work and research put into her eyesight, the prognosis looks good for an eventual full recovery." He then raised his glass to the table. "And most of all," he said as he took a moment to take in his audience, "to this family."

He stopped for a moment. It looked like emotion

was getting the better of him. He quickly collected himself and went on. "Because that is what we are now. . . . We are a family. Loki is gone. And for that. . . I feel nothing. Because my brother died twenty years ago. And I grieved for him with all my heart. But Loki. . . Loki's death is a blessing for everyone in this room. And I believe that he's taken with him all the pain and all the sorrow that he's caused us. I believe. . . no, I *know* that Loki's absence is the one thing that can mark a new beginning for all of us here at this table. Not just all of us as individuals, but all of us as a family. So. . . to my family. . . and you too, Ed."

The entire table laughed as they clinked their glasses. Tom drank down his small glass of wine, and the rest of them threw back their water.

"And now we eat!" Natasha announced, bouncing up from her chair as some real inklings of normalcy began to kick in.

Listening to the toast had helped. Gaia was finally starting to believe it now. She was finally finding the ability to breathe freely and actually *be* in this insanely storybook moment. This time as she looked around the table, she wasn't just seeing some lonely child's naive fantasy of togetherness projected like a hologram into the room. This time she could see a truly admirable father, a kind and caring woman who loved him, the beginnings of a real sister, and. . . an unbelievably cute boy. A rather stunning boy, actually, who was still gripping her hand under the table.

Once Gaia turned to him, she found that the rest of the table seemed to float away like an unmanned sailboat, leaving only her and Ed swimming alone in the water. And while the new beginning for this family was something of a miracle, one look at Ed and Gaia knew that there was a much more essential new beginning to tend to. A new beginning that needed to begin immediately.

Gaia shot up from the table, grabbed onto Ed's wrist, and tugged him down the hallway.

GAIA PULLED ED INTO THE BATHROOM

and slammed the door behind him, leaning her hands against the door on either side of his face. She was bubbling with deter- mination at this point. She was overflowing with **Creaky Drawbridge** it. Because the clouds of Gaia's life had finally parted for two seconds, and the heavens had opened wide, and the sun shone down, casting a golden haze over all that was usually decrepit and gray and hopeless. . . so she had to move fast. Because it could only be a matter of time (Hours? Maybe even minutes?) before the next train wreck hit. It was a clear-cut pattern. A curse that seemed to work like clockwork. So the goal was simple.

Extend that time in the sun for as long as possible. Ignore the repression, depression, regression, and digression—also known as big, fat, lard-assed intimacy issues—that always got in the way. Hold them at bay while the sun was still out. Before the timer started its countdown again.

"Whoa, there, Tiger—," Ed laughed, pressing his back against the bathroom door.

"Shhh." Gaia placed her finger to her lips. "You talk too much, Ed," she whispered.

"Gaia, your dad's right in the—"

"*Shhh.* Don't talk. Listen, okay? Have you seen a lot of time travel movies?"

"What?" Ed looked positively dumbfounded.

"*Time-travel movies,* Ed," she pressed. "Am I speaking Spanish? You know, the movies where there's this one particular point in time when some kind of cosmic temporal screwup happens and then the whole universe just veers off in the wrong direction into some horrible alternate universe where everything sucks, until our trusty hero goes back to that point in time when everything got completely screwy and sets the universe back on course?"

"Um. . ." Ed was searching Gaia's eyes for possible

signs of insanity. "Yeah," he said finally. "Yeah, I've seen some of those—"

"Okay," Gaia rushed, "and would you say you have a good imagination?"

Ed was still having a little trouble keeping up. "I . . . uh. . ."

"*Pretend*," Gaia pushed him. "Are you good at pretending?"

"Yeah, I guess I—"

"Good. Perfect. Great," Gaia said. "Okay, here's the deal, Ed. New beginning, okay? New beginning. We had a cosmic temporal screwup that morning. We skipped over to this horrible alternate universe the morning after our night together. The morning you got shot at."

"Okay. . . ?"

"Okay, so let's *fix* it. Let's go back to that morning *right now* and set things back on the right course, okay?"

"I—I, uh. . . ," Ed stammered.

"*Ed*," she snapped. "Work with me here. You've got to work with me. You know how my life goes. You know we've got to make the most of our time here in the bathroom."

"Okay, *yes*," Ed agreed. "Okay, it's that morning again. We're back in that morning. I'm coming back home with Bisquick and Aunt Jemima."

"Good," Gaia encouraged him. "I'm watching you from out your bedroom window, waiting for you to get back here."

"Okay. I *don't* get shot at."

"Correct. You *do not* get shot at," Gaia agreed. "And I just watch you walk into the building, and then I wait for you to walk back through your bedroom door."

Ed reached down to the knob of the bathroom door, opened it slightly, and slammed it shut. "Honey, I'm *home*," he called quietly to Gaia's face. "I brought everything we need for the panc—"

Gaia grabbed onto Ed's shoulders and kissed him, pouring all the combined passion of that morning and this evening, and all the mornings and evenings in between, into one kiss. That's where she would have been. That's where she should have been. Waiting at the door to pull him back into that bed.

She probed every part of his mouth with her own, pressing him back against the door as he reached his arms around her waist and lifted her off the floor.

"What took you so long?" she whispered.

"I had to get the breakfast rose," he whispered back, tickling the inside of her ear with his lips. "You can't have breakfast in bed without the breakfast rose."

And just like that, Gaia knew they weren't pretending anymore. They were there. They were in Ed's bedroom all those days ago, living out what should have been the rest of that morning. It was so easy to go back. Because in so many ways, she had never really left. The real Gaia had stayed in that room, while ignorant monkey Gaia raised in captivity just babbled and screamed a bunch of destructive nonsense in the miserable alternate universe. But they were back now. Back where they were supposed to be. And this time Gaia was going to talk. Repression was off-limits. Lying was off-limits. Just truth. As much of it as she could stuff into this one moment.

"I want to go back to bed," she told him.

"Yes," Ed agreed. "Pancakes later. Let's go back to bed."

"And then I want to go to the street fair down the street."

"*Yes.*" Ed laughed, pulling Gaia tighter to his body. "So do *I*. I want to go through boxes of two-dollar tube socks with you."

"I want to look at sushi refrigerator magnets with you, and bad mix tapes."

"I want a sausage sandwich and a chocolate crepe," Ed said. "And I want to stay there till they shut the damn thing down."

"Once I've eaten ten pounds of fried dough, we can leave," Gaia said. "And then back—"

"To bed, absolutely," Ed agreed.

Gaia brought her head back slowly, brushing her cheek against the stubble on Ed's chin, gently kissing the corner of his mouth and the area just above his lips. And then finally his lips, breathing him in and out and in again, feeling his fingertips running long trails along the skin of her stomach and her back.

"Ed," she whispered. "I want to look at tiny, crappy apartments with you, and get a giant dog with you, and read the paper with you, and any other boring bourgeois nonsense you can think of. . . with you."

"Is that a proposal?" Ed grinned. "Should I go ask your father for your hand?"

"What, do you think I'm a lunatic?" Gaia squawked. "I'm seventeen years old."

"Kidding," Ed said as he smacked his back up against the wall and grabbed Gaia by the shoulders. "Are you fully awake?" he asked, examining her eyes carefully.

Gaia stepped closer and leaned against him. And for the first time in her life, being fearless finally served a *truly* useful purpose. "I'm fully awake, Ed," she said, looking straight into his dark brown eyes. "And I'm in love with you."

And with those words, Gaia swore she could actually hear life falling back into alignment like a loud, creaky drawbridge.

Unfortunately, that wasn't the only thing she heard. Ed and Gaia both snapped their heads toward the door as a loud scream rang out from back down the hall.

Tell me it's a joke, Gaia said to herself as she whipped open the bathroom door and ran for the living room, Ed following close behind. *Tell me it was a laugh or the sound of someone being tickled. Just don't tell me the clouds are closing already. . . .*

Gaia leapt out into the living room. It was definitely not a joke. It was just a sight that she couldn't begin to understand.

Her father's face was turning a horrid shade of purple. His hands were clutching at his neck as his entire torso fell forward on the table, writhing in some kind of inexplicable pain.

"Somebody call an ambulance!" Natasha screamed.

"I just did!" Tatiana replied. "They're coming! They're coming now."

Gaia leapt to her father's side and tried to prop him up. "Are you choking?" she asked urgently.

He shook his head no and looked over at Natasha.

"Don't worry, Tom," Natasha cried. "The ambulance is on its way."

"I don't *understand*," Gaia shouted, looking into her father's desperate eyes. "I don't understand what happened!"

"Try to stay calm, Gaia," Natasha pleaded. "I'm sure the ambulance will—"

There was a loud pounding at the door. "EMS!" they barked through the door. "EMS. We got an emergency call—open up!"

The ambulance had already arrived. It was the fastest Gaia had ever seen an ambulance arrive on the scene.

SOMETHING'S GOING ON OUT THERE.

Something big has happened.

Daily Injection

At first he could tell just by the sounds. Suddenly all these chaotic sounds were pouring through the walls of his room. They'd always seemed to keep complete order out there before, but now men and soldiers were barking at each other like dogs. Engines were starting up one after the other as horns honked endlessly and tires dug into the dirt. But that was just the beginning.

He hoisted himself from his hospital bed, ignoring the awful pain in his chest, and stepped up next to the one small circular window by the sink. He'd thanked God every day for that window. At least they let him look at something other than his bed and those ugly cement walls and that one stupid little travel chessboard they'd let him have.

He crouched down and peered through the crud-covered one-foot window. And what he saw was the first glimmer of hope he'd had in weeks.

There was major movement. *Major.* These weren't the usual little practice ops he'd seen them working on before with the armored cars and the RVs. Cars and jeeps were lining up in droves as the men hollered out indecipherable orders to each other.

Jesus, they're moving out! This is some kind of

abandon-ship. He was sure of it. What else could it possibly be?

And then all the little pieces of the day started to make more sense. He hadn't had his usual visit from the doctor. They hadn't come in to give him his daily injection.

Wait a minute. Maybe that's why I'm so alert? Maybe that's why things are coming through so loud and clear today? No sedation. God, maybe this is it? Maybe this is my chance to break out of this place?

He tried to run to the door, but running was still a little tough on the chest wounds. He got to the door and tugged with as much strength as he could muster. But it was useless. The door was still locked shut. It didn't matter how much it looked like a cheap, shoddy hospital room; it was still just a prison cell in disguise.

All right, think, he ordered himself for the thousandth time while pacing around gingerly in the tiny cell. *Think this through. Play it like a game. Play it like a chess game.*

Of course, it looked like a stalemate, but *some* new move had just presented itself, he was sure of it. If they were really starting to ship out of the compound, then there had to be some new escape route opening up. Some area that was less guarded now or perhaps not even guarded at all?

Come on. Think of your maps.

He'd mapped whole quadrants of the compound in his head the few times they'd let him out of his cell for any reason. Even when he was still stuck on the gurney, he'd managed a few drowsy observations. Now he just had to turn his observations into a game of chess.

Come on. Picture the stalemate and find the way out.

He flashed back to an ugly stalemate he'd fallen into with Gaia one day at the park, and that left a horrible pain in his chest again. But this pain wasn't coming from his wounds. This was just that same horrid twinge he felt in his heart every time he thought of her. Which was about thirty to fifty times a day. Combined with his wounds, that equaled a whole lot of pain.

But if he could find his way back to her. . . If there really was a chance developing here, then for God's sake he had to take it, no matter what the risk. He certainly wasn't about to rot to death in this cell just dreaming about Gaia and the day that he'd finally be sitting across from her again in Washington Square Park in the rain. He'd had enough of that for one lifetime. *So think, you idiot. What's your next move? How the hell are you going to get home?*

He didn't have his exact answer yet, but he sure as hell had his motivation.

Just picture Gaia at the other end of the board and you'll get there. You will get there.

here is a sneak peek of Fearless™ #25: LOST

A fast-food
wrapper
skittered
across the
pathway in front **lab**
of him, its
bright red color **rat**
one of the most
beautiful
things he'd
ever seen.

HE WAS ABLE TO HEAR EVERYTHING.

After months of being trapped in this cold, white cell, he had trained himself to hear it all. Every turn of a key in a lock. Every click of a door. Every footstep. Every word. Every sneeze. Sometimes he even heard a breath. With nothing to see, nothing to smell, nothing to feel, his hearing became honed. Like that of a bat. Like a mouse. Like the lab rat he was.

White Room

There was something going on. New sounds. New words. New tones. Things were starting to fall apart, that much was clear. He could tell from the high pitch of his captors' voices. He could tell from the running. The quick clip-clop of their compulsively shined shoes.

He pressed his fingertips and palms up against the glass that closed him off from the sparkling white hall beyond. From the gleaming tile. From the one tiny crack in the plaster on the far wall that he'd studied so hard and for so long that it started to appear in his dreams. It was the only thing of discord in this sterile, regimented place. Until now.

Footsteps came. Rapidly. His heart hit his throat and he pressed his cheek against the glass, waiting. Suddenly a guard ran down the hall, zipping right past him in a blur of color. So close, yet so untouchable.

More voices.

"What are you going to do with them? You can't move them! We have strict orders to—"

"The orders don't matter anymore! We have to contain this!"

A third voice. A scared voice. Possibly the voice of Five Oh Three, the guard with the twitchy eye. "Let's just let them go! If the cops come here and find this place—"

Let them go! the prisoner thought, pressing his face so hard into the glass it hurt. *Yes! Let them go!*

"NO! We have our orders!"

"Aren't you listening to me! Loki's not coming back! He is as good as dead! Our orders don't matter anymore!

There was a loud clatter. A punch landed. A jaw cracked. A body hit the floor. The prisoner had a sinking feeling that Five Oh Three would have been his only ally. He swallowed hard. If Loki was as good as dead, wasn't he as well? Would the morons out there even bother to continue to feed him? Would he rot away in this white room for the rest of his numbered days?

The moment the prisoner stepped back from the glass, Four Five Seven appeared at the side of his cell. Four Five Seven was the round-jawed, pudgy, yet strong Hispanic guard who brought the prisoner his injections. Who held him down while Four Nine Two and Five Oh Three administered the serums. He'd never known his captors by their real names, only by

3

the numbers embroidered in gold thread along their collars.

The prisoner narrowed his eyes as Four Five Seven silently raised the glass wall by remote control and entered his cell. Before he could formulate some kind of reason for this unexpected visit, Four Five Seven drew his gun from his holster and leveled it at the prisoner's heart.

"What's going on?" the prisoner asked calmly.

"You're moving," said Four Five Seven as he lifted the gun half an inch. "Now step out into the hall and make a right. I'll be right behind you and there's nowhere to go but straight, so don't try running."

The prisoner's pulse was racing like a thoroughbred's. Was this actually happening? Was he going to move outside the four walls of his tiny cell? He tentatively stepped past Four Five Seven, never taking his eyes off the gun until he was in the hall. It was colder out here. The air was crisper. Sweeter. It was a whole new smell and his nostrils actually prickled. He almost closed his eyes to savor it, but stopped himself.

"Move it," Four Five Seven ordered.

He walked down the hall, past the other cells. Some were empty. One held a girl, a redhead, who cowered in the corner, rocking back and forth. One held an older man, stooped and tired. He looked up as they passed, his blue eyes hopeful. Why were these people here? What was their offense? Was it merely loving someone, too? Was that all they had done?

The hallway opened onto a larger room where Five Oh Three was just struggling to his feet. A bruise was already forming on his left cheek.

"I thought I put you down," Four Five Seven said to the smaller man, still keeping his gun trained on the prisoner.

Five Oh Three looked the prisoner over. His eye twitched once. "Just let them go," he said again.

The prisoner looked at Four Five Seven, who tightened his grip on the gun. "We can't let them go," he said. "We have orders."

"Fine," Five Oh Three said. Then, faster than the prisoner ever would have thought possible, Five Oh Three ripped his gun from his holster and blasted off a shot, sending Four Five Seven reeling backwards.

The prisoner stood there for a moment, stunned and free, as Four Five Seven's gun clattered to the floor. The wound was in his shoulder, but it was bleeding like a geyser. The guard didn't even shout out. He simply looked surprised.

"Well?" Five Oh Three said, the twitch wild now. "Run, you idiot!"

That was all he needed. The prisoner took off through a door at the far end of the room. There was another hallway and a guard came running toward him from the other end. He raised his arms and kept running, ready to give the man a swift elbow to the jaw if he tried to stop him, but the guard sped past him as if he weren't even there.

The next door opened up into a brightly lit room that was three stories high and made almost entirely of glass. He blinked against the harshness of the light, momentarily incapacitated by it. Until he realized it was sunlight. Until he realized that those appalled things on the other side of the glass were trees.

Salivating now, he careened toward the exit door, across a marble floor dotted with black speckles and trimmed with gold. Every second he expected someone to jump out and tackle him to that floor. Every moment he expected to hear a shot ring out or a voice call for him to stop. But nothing came. There was no one. And in moments, he was tasting fresh air.

Outside he found himself feeling almost drunk. There were birds. There was wind. There was grass and asphalt. A fast-food wrapper skittered across the pathway in front of him, its bright red color one of the most beautiful things he'd ever seen.

A slam sounded from the compound behind him and he realized that he had to keep moving. He wasn't safe yet. He ran toward the woods that bordered the building. Ran until the branches had ripped through the soles of his soft slippers. He spotted a large rock and collapsed behind it, pressing his back up against its cool, uneven surface.

His breath was harsh and ragged. He hadn't had this much exercise in months and it made his heart pound dangerously. He sat for a moment and waited, gasping as quietly as possible. Listening. Waiting for the army that he was sure would be sent after him. They couldn't really all be gone. Most of them had to be there still. And when they realized what Five Oh Three had done, they would deal with him and come after the refugee.

He waited. He waited until his breathing normalized. Until his nose stopped running. Until his fingers were so cold he could barely curl them.

But no one was coming.

He stood and started to run again, cutting through the woods, just hoping he was going the right way. All he needed was a road. That, at least would be a start. He almost laughed when he heard traffic up ahead. He was on his way. He was on his way back to her.

Buffy the Vampire Slayer™

"Well, we could grind our enemies into powder with a sledgehammer, but gosh, we did that last night."

—Xander

As long as there have been vampires, there has been the Slayer. One girl in all the world, to find them where they gather and to stop the spread of their evil...the swell of their numbers.

LOOK FOR A NEW TITLE EVERY MONTH!

Based on the hit TV series created by
Joss Whedon

2400

Everyone's got his demons....

ANGEL™

If it takes an eternity, he will make amends.

Original stories based
on the TV show
Created by Joss Whedon
& David Greenwalt

Available from Simon Pulse
Published by Simon & Schuster

SIMON
PULSE

2311-01